SHOW-OFFS

SHOW-OFFS

GAY EROTIC STORIES

Edited by
Richard Labonté

Published in the United States by Cleis Press Inc.,
2246 Sixth Street, Berkeley, California 94710.

Printed in the United States.
Cover design: Scott Idleman/Blink
Cover photograph: Image Source
Text design: Frank Wiedemann
First Edition.
10 9 8 7 6 5 4 3 2 1

Trade paper ISBN: 978-1-57344-817-8
E-book ISBN: 978-1-57344-943-4

For Asa...
Thanks for staring at me,
all those years ago.

Contents

INTRODUCTION: THE WATCHERS AND THE WATCHED

Some men like to watch, and some men like to be watched. The universe has a way of balancing things out, doesn't it?

We're not talking sidewalk cruising here, that natural inclination for one man to appreciate another man's body in passing, perhaps leading to full-on sex, perhaps fueling, once he's alone, a climactic fantasy.

No, the stories in this collection are more furtive: the desired body savored voyeuristically through a window, through a crack in the closet door, through a camera lens, sometimes from right across the room; the body desired flaunting manly wares while bathing in a river, playing in a bathhouse, wearing a leaving-nothing-to-the-imagination thong.

Forget "like": some men *need* to be watched; some men *need* to watch. These are their stories.

My story: I was never really a watcher—a cruiser, of course, what gay man isn't, even if he hasn't acknowledged a gay bone (or boner) in his body. But in retrospect, I guess I was watched.

I worked retail for many years, clerking at and then managing A Different Light, a lesbian and gay bookstore that at one time had four stores. The first opened in the Silver Lake neighborhood of Los Angeles in 1979. That's where (and when) I met Rhonda-a-Go-Go. (Hey, it was the era of the Radical Faeries, and we all had alter egos; mine will never be revealed.) He'd come into the store and hang around; eventually I figured out he was flirting; we were lovers for a few years, have been friends for more than thirty. That's where, in 1983, I met Fernando, son of Mexican immigrants, University of Southern California film graduate, political activist. He'd come into the store and hang around; eventually I figured out he was flirting; we were together through his HIV, until 1990.

In 1987 I moved to San Francisco to take over management of the store on Castro Street. That's where I met Asa, a few years later. He'd come in from the bustling sidewalk, walk quickly through the store to the outside back patio, sit for a while in that quiet space, then wander around the store; for a while, staff figured him for a shoplifter, but after a couple of months he was relegated to the doesn't-buy, likes-to-browse, quirky-guy category.

Turns out—he was watching, I was watched—he came in to be around me, which we figured out eventually. We've been around each other now for twenty years. Voyeurism has its benefits....

Richard Labonté
Bowen Island, British Columbia

VACANCY

Jamie Freeman

I'm hiding out quietly, living in the historic center of a small Southern town, far away from home and politics and the growing craziness of Washington, DC. This place is *Sling Blade* come to life: towering, untamed azaleas; ancient Live Oaks entombed in shrouds of Spanish moss; brick-paved streets; rotting palm trees and shuttered mansions built to withstand Negro uprisings and hurricanes. Tonight it's raining hard as the outer bands of Hurricane Philippe begin to breach the town limits.

I'm sitting in my living room waiting for a visitor.

I moved into this neighborhood on the recommendation of one of the evening clerks at the hotel. She knew nothing about me, but I suspect even her countrified gaydar pinged when I walked into the lobby with my black vintage overcoat, carefully manicured hands and artfully haphazard haircut. She pointed listlessly in the direction of Lee Gardens and popped her gum in annoyance. "The Gardens," as the natives call them, are a dozen close-packed blocks huddled north of the old downtown named after the defeated hero of the conflict they refer to as simply, "the War." The Gardens are now populated mostly by academics, homosexuals and wealthy liberals, or as people here refer interchangeably to the three groups: "them Jews."

I rode through on my bike, eyeballing the big subdivided mansions, carriage-house apartments and tiny cottages sprinkled between the true jewels of the neighborhood: the privately owned mansions with perfect lawns and driveways crowded with BMWs, SUVs, and upmarket hybrids. *This could be okay*, I thought. And then I swerved to avoid a squirrel and smashed my bike against the curb, flying into the air and slamming down hard on the sidewalk. I skidded three feet, tearing the skin from my left forearm, and slamming my shoulder into the dirt.

I looked up.

I saw a mangled bicycle tire, a smear of bright-red blood on the sidewalk and a VACANCY sign on the lawn.

I was home.

I signed a lease and moved my belongings—two old suitcases and half a dozen cardboard boxes—from the Holiday Inn in my rented Prius. When I'd lugged everything upstairs, I stood in the middle of an empty apartment watching the mismatched ceiling fans turn in perfect unison. The wood floors, high ceilings and large windows were comforting after weeks in cheap, low-ceilinged motel rooms.

An empty apartment behind a couple of solid deadbolts worked for me.

I bought a television, a DVD player and a blood-red sleeper sofa.

My apartment occupied the entire second floor of an old house that might once have been a single-family dwelling, but which, judging from the bathroom and kitchen fixtures, has been subdivided for at least sixty years. A narrow inside stairwell led down to a private door that opened into the side yard. Behind my apartment there was another second-floor apartment across a narrow alley. Smaller than mine, this one was perched atop an old dilapidated carriage house that I was surprised could support the weight of all that plaster, wood and tile.

The neighborhood was the product of another age. Unlike the sprawling McMansions in the new subdivisions on the edge of town, separated by acreage and high fences, these houses were built right on top of one another. Houses like these were built in a time when privacy was an attitude of omission, rather than a marketable amenity; when neighbors pretended not to hear the crying or screaming or moaning of others who lived nearby. The houses predated air-conditioning and had never been modernized, so the sounds of my neighbors drifted into my life on the summer breeze, chopped up and rained down on me by the ceiling fans that turned restlessly overhead. We all lived in the past, crowded together through the murderous heat of the Southern summer.

My first night in the apartment I'd been awakened from an early evening nap by the syncopated music and moans of a pornographic movie radiating up through the floorboards of the back bedroom. I bundled up a bag of garbage and crept quietly downstairs and out into the side yard. I wandered around the corner of the house and peeked in the window of my downstairs neighbor's bedroom. I could see the giant television, dominated by a close-up of a very thick cock plunging back and forth through the pink lips of a vagina that pulsed and gripped the shaft like something alive and hungry. I could see long hairy legs stretched out on the bed. This must be Robert—the "hot faggot downstairs from you"—whose sexual orientation the landlord's rat-haired secretary had apparently misjudged.

He had nice legs and feet, for a straight guy.

But the angle of the window prevented me from seeing more of his body.

I took a step closer and the head of his cock bobbed into view, bouncing above the rhythmic pounding of his hand. I could hear him whispering, "Yeah, baby," and "Oh, yeah, come on, baby," as he jacked himself.

I took another step; now I could see the entire length of his cock. My heart was thumping and my throat was beginning to constrict. My cock strained against the inside of my loose exercise shorts. I reached down inside my pants, grasping my hard shaft and giving it a gentle tug. I glanced around me; I could be seen from the street, but at this hour the street was dark and empty. Inside I heard Robert say, "Yeah, yeah, now bring it home, come on, baby, bring it home." His hand sped up.

I pushed the elastic band of my running shorts down below my cock, hooking it under my balls and jacking myself with a growing sense of urgency. I heard Robert's voice, a little louder than before, saying, "Oh, god," and then I saw cum spurting from the end of his cock. I watched the huge gobs of cum, imagining it raining down onto a tight belly and a thin, hard chest, and I came in a burst of thin, ropy spurts that shot out and down onto the damp soil at my feet. I watched Robert's hand moving lazily up and down the length of his rod, coaxing out every last bit of cum, the tiny glistening pearls dropping down from the spongy head of his cock and mixing with the lubrication on his hand.

I stepped back quietly, tucking my cock back inside my shorts and hurrying to the oversized county-issue garbage can he and I shared.

As I walked back past the window, I glanced into Robert's

bedroom. He was standing in front of the television facing the window, still stroking his huge cock, coaxing it into another erection. Behind him, backlighting his little show, a moaning woman with French tips was fingering her labia and saying, "Come on, Daddy, put that big thing inside me."

I was startled by the hungry, vacant look in his eyes.

I blushed and looked away, but Robert's gaze followed me down the path to my door and inside my apartment.

That night I dreamed that Robert chased me naked across the yard, tackled me in the mud, straddled my shoulders with his powerful thighs and face-fucked me until I woke up gasping for air and shooting cum into my sweat-drenched sheets.

It was almost three in the morning, but the sounds of cheap music and syncopated grunting were still oozing up through the floorboards from Robert's bedroom.

I spent an hour standing under a cold shower trying to drown the phantom sensation of his cock slamming against the back of my throat.

Later in the week I saw Robert again, smiling and chatting up MY NAME IS MIRANDA at the Vegan Vixen, a trendy sandwich shop in the next block. I stood aloof from the pair, ordering a sandwich disingenuously listed on the chalkboard menu as the SEITAN CLUB and waiting while the hulking goth in the kitchen packed my order. I heard a cough and glanced up; Robert grinned and nodded in my direction.

I nodded back, my face burning in remembrance of our previous meeting.

Later that evening I was home pacing barefoot in front of the giant windows of my apartment, drinking cheap whiskey from the bottle and chain-smoking. "Big Brother" was playing on the television and I was half-listening to the bickering housemates. I saw Robert's BMW screech to a halt downstairs, one tire climbing the curb in front of the house. Robert and Miranda tumbled out opposite sides of the car; I could hear Robert laughing and talking. He glanced up at my window and I stepped back into the shadows, feeling the hot sting of his gaze on my cheek like a slap.

I dropped on the couch and heard Robert's front door slam. They were laughing and they sounded drunk; I could hear Robert's voice rumbling and sexy beneath her annoying high-pitched giggles. They stayed in the front room for a while and then moved back to the bedroom. I stood up and walked back to the empty bedroom above Robert's, standing in silence in the dark room. The air was hot and still, but I left the ceiling fan off, silent and motionless above my head.

With no carpet to absorb the sounds, I could hear their voices clearly enough: his coaxing, hers high and coquettish. They did a verbal dance that went on too long. I was considering going back to the living room when I heard Robert's voice. "Oh, yeah, baby, you're so tight."

I was instantly erect, my cock bouncing at the sound of his voice, pitched loud; he knew I could hear him.

Robert talked and talked; an endless narration of his actions that provoked only the occasional, barely audible response from Miranda. "Oh, yeah, baby, my cock is so big, it's like I'm splitting you apart," and "*Ooh*, take it all inside." Then Robert started saying, "You're not done bitch, get back over here." I could hear her laughing or crying and he was grunting and then, when a sharp slap rang out in the hot stillness, I shot like a cannon, cum flying across the room and splattering the window that faced the back alley.

I stifled a groan, listening as Robert vocalized below me, groaning and grunting. More laughing or crying from the girl and I kept jacking myself, coaxing more and more cum from my helpless, heaving cock.

And that's when I realized there was someone watching from the window across the alley. A shadowy figure—visible only as a shifting of light and dark—moved away from the window, disappearing from my line of sight. I knew it was dark in my own apartment, but the glow of the moon illuminated the back alley trash cans and the branches that scraped against my windows. I wondered how much the shadowy figure had seen. The idea of this unanticipated attention gave me another erection, which I had just about worked through when Robert's voice drifted up from below, "Come on, baby, let me fuck you up the ass."

I'd been living in the apartment for a month when I saw my neighbor from across the alley again. It was late, sometime after three in the morning, and I'd fallen asleep naked on the sofa, the remains of a righteous masturbation session dried across my hairy stomach. I'd been awakened when the DVD stopped spinning and the player had finally powered down, switching the television back to a full-volume infomercial. I lurched up, feeling around for the remote.

I wrestled with the volume and left the television flickering quietly as I wandered into the kitchen for something to drink. I left the overhead light off, but leaned over to root around in the refrigerator for a bottle of Evian. When I straightened up, I cracked the lid and downed half the bottle in one gulp, letting the cool bubbling liquid run down my chin, my neck and my chest.

I paused, pulling the bottle back from my mouth, still standing in the cool, bright light from the refrigerator, letting the chilled air slide across my hot skin. I caught a movement out of the corner of my eye. I turned and saw a dark figure in the window across the alley. I could make out little more than a dark outline, backlit by yellowish light. The broad shoulders and slim hips gave the impression of masculinity, as did the slow, back-and-forth motion of one of the arms. It took a few minutes for me to register what was happening.

The stranger in the window was beating off. I stood and watched, willing my eyes to adjust and let the image of the masturbating man resolve into recognizable lines, but it was too dark. I watched the shadowy outline as the arm sped up perceptibly for a few seconds. A heavy grunt drifted toward me through the window screen. The man's shoulders hunched forward, his knees flexing as he bent over to milk the last of his seed onto the floor at his feet. Everything was dark; my imagination was struggling to create images to match the sounds my ears were hearing.

There was a long moment of stillness and then the figure turned and walked away. As he moved, light played across a strongly muscled torso and a pendulous, low hanging cock. I was so startled by his size and physical perfection that my bottle of water slipped from my fingers, bouncing on the tile with a plastic thunk and spraying sparkling French spring water all over the tile at my feet.

I glanced down at my own semierect cock in stunned silence and then glanced back across the back alley. I had a line of sight that drew my eye shotgun-style through three rooms to the far end of the apartment. A single lamp burned in the front room, but the apartment was silent and still.

I took my cock in my hand and jacked it for a while watching the empty apartment, thinking of the outline of muscular arms, the flash of light across clearly defined pecs and the glimpse of thick cock hanging loosely between the slim thighs. I tossed out a quick spurt of cum—its volume diminished by my earlier endeavors—that dropped to the floor and mixed with the spilled Evian.

I spent night after night smoking and pacing and watching the apartment behind mine.

Robert's performances provided a regular respite from my other spying; most evenings at some point I found myself standing in the bushes outside his window watching him. Sometimes he would watch bisexual porn, shooting streams of jizz across his abs just as one of the men entered the other from behind, or saying, "Oh, yeah, fuck him you big stud," then edging until the muscular top pulled out and came across the bottom's bouncing backside. Robert would groan and pump and let his own spray echo the action on the screen. I pondered the invitation implicit in this new video subject matter, but although Robert knew I was standing behind him, jerking off in the darkness, clearly visible sometimes in the mirror over his dresser, he never did more than glance in my direction.

Apparently all he wanted was an audience.

And that worked for me.

In the intermissions between Robert's spirited performances, I stood vigil upstairs, watching across the alley, looking for movement, but seeing nothing. There was evidence of habitation: lights turned on and off, items appearing and disappearing from the kitchen counter; clean plates or glasses stacked in the drying rack next to the sink, but I never saw my neighbor.

During the afternoons when the sun slanted down through the high windows of the apartment behind me, I had a clear view of most of the living room, the whole kitchen and what looked like a spare—or at least unused—bedroom. I pulled my binoculars out of a cardboard box I'd never bothered to unpack and meticulously swept the room looking for clues to the identity of my neighbor. The place was nearly as empty as my own apartment. Boxes were piled here and there, along with an old record player and a stack of records, a futon, an ancient television and, in the spare bedroom, a bare mattress and box spring. Nondescript mugs, plates and glasses were stacked in the kitchen. The only item that seemed to hint at the personality of the person living in the house was an enormous movie poster—Arthur Penn's *Bonnie and Clyde*—tacked up over the futon. On the coffee table there was an expensive digital camera and a row of carving knives, neatly arranged from shortest to longest.

I spent hours staring into the semidarkness of the neighboring apartment, waiting for darkness and shadowy movement.

I'd been living in the Gardens for a month when the approach of a late-season hurricane intruded on my solitude. At the hysterical insistence of the local television anchors, I ventured out into the world in search of storm supplies.

The sky was blue and still, brilliant and ominously empty.

The streets and yards around my apartment were empty as well, the cars having transported their owners north in anticipation of the mandatory evacuation orders that would come too late. Yards had been stripped of ornaments and the houses themselves had been boarded up, their façades obscured by sheets of blond plywood.

Robert's car was gone.

I walked through the empty streets, thinking of the end of the world.

I discovered a hive of activity surrounding the local Home Depot, where I watched people loading supplies indiscriminately into orange plastic carts. "He looks like a big one," an elderly woman said, taking down a dozen packs of batteries and tossing them into her cart. "Philippe's gonna be the biggest hurricane to ever hit this area," the checkout girl told me as she rang up my stack of batteries and a long, black Maglite.

I walked past shuttered grocery stores and fast-food restaurants, stopping at a neighborhood gas station to buy cigarettes and cereal. I paid nine-fifty for the last bottle of spring water in the place.

I walked back to my house as the rain started to fall.

I fumbled for my key, but found the door unlocked. I stared at the doorknob for a long time, then pulled my Maglite out of the bag and started up the dark stairs to my apartment, leaving my packages on the front stoop.

The apartment was empty, but there was a note taped to the back-facing window of the bedroom above Robert's room. I could look beyond it into the living room of the apartment behind me. The note said: *I'm cumming for you*. The ambiguous words, written in plain block letters, sent a chill down my spine. Was this from Robert? Or the knife-collecting muscleman?

I stared at the note until a crack of thunder startled me out of my trance.

The rain became heavier, pounding the roof and lashing against the windows as Hurricane Philippe crawled closer.

I hauled my shopping bags up the stairs and left the front door unlocked.

I paced, smoking and watching the Weather Channel.

Outside the storm began to rage. Branches and debris slammed against the roof. Somewhere in the distance I heard the sound of a window shattering. The power flickered.

I watched a hundred-and-fifty-year-old oak topple over in the wind, smashing through the roof of the house across the street.

When the power finally failed, I stripped off my clothes and sat naked on the sofa.

The darkness magnified the sounds of the storm.

I reached down and started stroking myself.

I heard the door at the base of the stairs fly open, the wind funneling wet leaves up from below and then stopping suddenly as the front door closed.

My cock sprang to life in my hand, a bead of precum oozing out onto my fingers.

I heard footsteps, heavy on the stairs.

I waited in the darkness, my cock erect in anticipation.

IN THE EYE OF THE BEHOLDER (WELL, ALMOST)

Tony Pike

This story tells of things that happened some thirty years ago, at a time when, unlike today, no gay man had to sheathe himself in rubber when he fucked his fellow man...

Gary, just turned eighteen, was in his last year at boarding school. So was his wank buddy of three weeks' standing, Tom, though he was a year older than Gary and had a cock size to prove it. They were on their way, this Saturday afternoon, to the cliff-top hideaway among the thorn bushes that had become their special place for doing together what they enjoyed most: pulling their trousers down in the open air and fiercely pulling on each other's cock until they'd both shot their loads. As they walked along this afternoon they were already half stiff inside their trousers in anticipation, but as they were still on the public pathway they had to content themselves with sticking a hand into the other's pocket and feeling for his slippery dick.

There would still be a minute or two before they reached

their secret spot. *Time for a question*, Gary thought. "You know," he began, and his voice came out husky and tremulous, "when two guys have sex together—I don't mean what we do, I mean when they actually fuck—how do they...I mean, how do they exactly...go about it?"

"Well," Tom answered, his voice also a bit unsteady now, "I'm not sure I really know." His fingers, unbidden, jiggled Gary's cock through the thin fabric of his trouser pocket. "I've never really thought about it." (Gary doubted that but let it pass.) "I suppose—I imagine—that if they did it in a bed, or on a bed, then one would lie flat on his tummy and spread his legs a bit, and the other would lie on top and—er—poke in his prick."

"And would the other one come, do you think, while he was being fucked? Or would he wait his turn and fuck the other one afterward?"

"You think a guy might come while he was being fucked? You mean without touching himself?"

"I don't know. It's a possibility, isn't it? Maybe the friction, as his body was pushed forward on the sheets with the motion of the fuck?" Gary thought back to the time—mere weeks ago—when the only way he'd known how to come was by rubbing his stubby penis against the woolly cover of his bed. How long ago that seemed! How much experience he seemed to have collected since!

"Maybe," said Tom thoughtfully. "Maybe being fucked does make men come. I really have no idea. Maybe the underneath one simply sticks his hand down under his belly and gives himself a wank."

"Or the one on the top could, I suppose," said Gary, his mind forming delicious pictures of the alternative scenarios they were conjuring up. He felt himself harden a bit more against Tom's fingers, which were still fiddling in his pocket.

"Well, here we are," announced Tom, his voice now shaky and almost gulping with lust. The narrowness of the path forced him to extricate his hand from Gary's pocket, and Gary had similarly to let go, as Tom began to lead the way between the springing bushes, parting them for Gary to follow easily as he went. Then suddenly he turned to Gary and hissed urgently in his ear. "Get down, we're not alone."

"What?" Gary whispered back.

"Get down. Lie flat. Inch forward on your tummy. You'll soon see."

Gary did as he was told. Side by side they slid on their bellies through the grass and yellow flowering fennel, their rigid and forward-pointing pricks slightly impeding their progress and giving them further cause for caution and care.

The place they were making for, the little clearing among the high fennel flowers, with its long view across the sea, was already occupied. Two young men—probably in their early twenties, Gary guessed—had got there first. They were making bolder use of the place than Tom and Gary ever had. They were totally naked. And they were fucking. Actually fucking. Two grown men together were here in the clearing, in the middle of having a fuck. And Tom and Gary had arrived just in time to watch.

The bottom one (there really wasn't a better word) was kneeling forward, his elbows and his forehead on the ground, his rounded rump raised high. The other man knelt behind, between his legs, also proudly naked and with torso almost upright, gleaming with sweat as he rode his friend. Occasionally he put out a hand to steady himself, either against the ground or his partner's golden back, as he rammed his cock into the bottom one's bottom. Discarded clothes lay in neglected disarray all around the clearing—though Gary and Tom barely noticed those.

They watched in almost frozen disbelief. The top man's bum was peach-like yet mobile, flexing its muscles as it pistoned to and fro. Both men were fit-looking and lightly tanned, neither had much body hair. But it wasn't even these fine features that were the boys' main foci of attention. Nor was it the thick and floppy mop of dark-blond hair the bottom one wore, nor the straight raven plumes of the top guy, that swung to and fro in a sweat-matted mane as he thrust his way toward his climax. It was the amazing view they both had, because they were watching the scene sideways on, and from just a few inches above the ground, and barely three feet away, of the two men's hammering, pulsing dicks.

The young man doing the fucking (Raven-Hair) showed his only intermittently, and even then not the whole length of it, as it slid in and out, in and out of Floppy-Mop's hole. Even so, Gary could see that it was a mighty one, a sight such as he had never seen. Even Tom's grand penis (Gary had measured it and made it seven inches and a quarter) would be dwarfed by this. It had a curve to it; it seemed to go on and on; impossible to see if it was circumcised or not, but it thickened toward the base. And as it alternately pulled halfway out and plunged back in, so the tight round scrotum that hung around that base rode back and forth, slamming between the other's buttock-cheeks so hard that Gary found himself wondering if it hurt.

Then there was the other man's. Floppy-Mop he might be but no way floppy-cocked. There it was in full view and close-up, suspended below its owner's belly, and very stiff, so that it pressed up against the belly, only occasionally jerking away from it in time with the impact of Raven-Hair's harder slams. It wasn't very long. Considering the age and size of its owner, that is. Gary, the expert now, would have estimated it at a little short of six inches: considerably shorter than Tom's, though just as thick. Gary found that lack of length reassuring. He whose own endowment came out at five and a half. Grown men didn't all have to be giants in the dick department then. They could still have plenty of fun with sex.

Floppy-Mop's penis had a foreskin, though. Gary couldn't help noticing that from where he lay motionless, his body pressed down on his own ramrod of a hard-on, just a couple of feet away. And Floppy-Mop's foreskin was a long and ample one, not pushed far back by his state of erection, and so only giving a tantalizing glimpse of the damson-colored tip beneath.

Then, with Gary's and Tom's eyes fixed on it, it shot. No hand was near it, neither its owner's nor that of the still plunging Raven-Hair. Yet Floppy-Mop was able to shoot his load without any such external help. In full view of the watching boys his bursting dick gave a quiver, swelled, opened its little hole and squirted a thick white jet of come. It flew out in an arcing line that landed on the ground right by the young man's face. He gave a gasp. "I've shot," he said breathlessly to Raven-Hair, as another thick spurt followed the first (such quantities Gary had never seen before now, even pouring forth from Tom) and then the remainder of his load tumbled more slowly out of his dick and fell drooling to the ground beneath.

Raven-Hair reached a hand underneath his friend as if to check that what he'd said was true. He massaged the still oozing dick to help the last droplets find their way out. And then it seemed as though Raven-Hair was coming too. He pushed in hard and Floppy-Mop beneath him collapsed to the ground. All there was to be seen now was Raven-Hair's squirming peachy bum as he drove home his last few thrusts to an accompaniment of grunts.

"I think I'm going to come," Gary whispered urgently to Tom. But Tom did not reply. Because—as Gary was shortly to see—there was no time. To Gary's amazement Tom rose up from his camouflaged position among the fennel plants and grass, knelt up, coming into view of the two suddenly alarmed young men, rapidly fumbled his school trousers open—his cock exploded out of his fly and he took it urgently in his hand—but for no more than a second before his sperm came flying out.

Gary found himself almost unbelieving of what Tom had just done. It was so out of character for lovely Tom, cautious about being seen or getting caught, yet here he was now, brazenly kneeling to attention, facing two young men (who were now rooted to the spot, mouths agape in astonishment) with his cock out and spraying a shower of milky drops that spattered in every direction at once, so frantic was the motion of his fist.

Little by little the astonished expressions of the two immobile young men naked on the grass in front of them changed. From fear and horror they turned to relief, even amusement, though that was still tempered by some vestige of surprise. Raven-Hair, lying on top, was able to twist his body some way round toward them, though his weapon stayed buried up to the hilt inside Floppy-Mop, who remained skewered to the ground as firmly as any butterfly transfixed by a pin on a collector's board.

"What have we here," said Raven-Hair, now grinning toward Tom. (Gary he had not yet seen.) "A nice big lad with a nice big dicky."

At this point Gary was at last overwhelmed by everything that had been happening and knew that he couldn't hold off any longer. Following the precedent set by Tom he too rose to his knees, unzipping while he did so, and out, predictably, sprang his five-and-a-half-inch knob, like a lively fat lizard.

The eyes of both men darted at once toward the sudden new arrival on the scene and toward Gary's up-springing cock in particular. "Hey," said Floppy-Mop, peering around Raven-

Hair's left arm, "and he's brought his little friend with him."

Gary had even less time to get his hand involved than Tom had. Didn't even get as far as touching it. He felt his cock let fly—a sudden automatic catapult—and then all watched in amazement as his load arced out and up, like a harpoon line, then curved down, to land an inch in front of the startled Floppy-Mop's nose. Floppy-Mop flinched and blinked his thickly lashed blue eyes. "Hey, wow," he said. "The little guy may not have a big one yet, but he sure has a way of making up for it!"

"You certainly did surprise me," said Gary on their walk back to school, as they were talking over what had just happened. "I mean, getting up like that and showing yourself off to them, bold as brass."

"Hm," said Tom. Did he flush slightly pink, or did Gary just imagine that? "You can hardly talk, doing exactly the same a moment later."

"Only because you did," Gary countered, laughing.

"At least I didn't nearly put someone's eye out with my shoot," said Tom, "unlike someone I could mention."

Not much had happened after Gary had so spectacularly delivered his load. All four of them had just come, after all. Raven-Hair had pulled his long, long organ out of his friend's behind. Then both pairs of boys had shuffled a foot or two toward each other, and played for a moment with each others' spent organs with their hands. (*I'm holding a twenty-year-old's cock in my hands*, Gary thought in near-disbelief, as he fondled first Floppy-Mop's standard-size equipment, and then Raven-Hair's majestic hose. Never mind that they weren't up for action at that precise moment. He'd seen them both in splendid operation just three minutes before.)

Floppy-Mop said to Gary, "Sorry about calling you little just now. That was only in comparison with your big friend here—with his lovely big thing. You've got a good strong dick for a kid of your age. Believe me, it'll grow into something quite special before too long. Maybe even bigger than your friend's." He gave Tom's still stiff penis a conspiratorial squeeze. "I'd like to see it when it does." He had smiled then at them both.

After that, Gary and Tom had stuffed their slippery organs back inside their trousers, while the older two got up and put their clothes back on. With vague noises about "seeing you again some time," the two pairs of boys, or young men, had split and gone off in opposite directions along the cliff path.

The following Saturday Tom was away, on a weekend home visit. Left to his own devices Gary found himself walking along the familiar cliff-top path. He told himself he had no particular idea in mind, although he'd taken the trouble to dress in his running kit—white T-shirt and shorts (with nothing underneath) and plimsolls without socks. He pushed his way through the bushes toward the spot where he'd seen and learned so much a week before. No one was there. Gary sat on the grass and looked out at the glassy sea a hundred feet below. Absently he reached down and began to undo his shorts...

"Hey there! Hallo." Startled, and beginning to blush, Gary looked around. A young man had shouldered his way through the bushes and stood looking down at him as he sat on the cliff edge from just a yard away. And Gary recognized him.

"We met before," said the young man. "Remember? Last week. At this very spot."

"Too right we did," said Gary. He was looking at, and talking to, the young blond man with the floppy mop of hair whom he'd watched being fucked, and ejaculating, just where he was sitting now. "And we..." He felt his blush turning from pink to puce.

"Yes," said Floppy-Mop blithely. "And very—er—stimulating it was too." He grinned broadly. "But there were two of you then, and now you're on your own."

"There were two of you that day too," Gary countered, awkwardly doing up his shorts with one hand and trying to look as if he wasn't.

"Well, Alex is away this weekend. And my name's Peter, by the way. I've got a place near here." He gestured with an arm away from the sea, across the field, toward a line of nondescript houses. "One of those is where I live. I share with Alex and another bloke. We're all students at art school." He looked at Gary in silence for a moment, weighing up the possibilities, and thinking what to do or say next. And Gary looked steadily back at him, waiting for him to give a lead. Peter screwed up his courage. "Do you want to come back with me? If you've got time. It's not like I live alone. Alex is away but the other guy, Simon's in. It's not that you'd have to worry if you were safe. As there's two of us in the house."

Gary looked at his watch. "I'm supposed to be back at school at four..."

"It's only just after two now. You'd have plenty of time to see the place, have a cup of coffee, do anything else we felt like doing...if we felt like doing it...and still get back for four. And you'd know where to come if you ever wanted to come again." Seeing a smile on Gary's face, Peter amended, "Well, you know what I meant to say."

"Perhaps you meant to say more than one thing at a time," Gary said, getting to his feet, and thought he'd been quite clever.

They set off across the edge of the field to where the line of rooftops Peter had pointed to marked the beginning of the outskirts of the town. "We go this way, in through the back garden," Peter said. "And what's your name, by the way? If you want to tell me, that is."

"No harm in a name," Gary answered. He felt sure he could trust this man. He'd seen him being fucked, after all, seven days ago, and felt his cock, and Peter had gently felt his too. "I'm Gary," he said. "My friend, who you saw, is Tom. He's away for the weekend too."

Peter was wearing old, belted jeans, quite tight around the bum, enabling Gary to note approvingly the round fullness of that bum's cheeks. He remembered with a little private smile the rather better view of them he'd had when Peter was being fucked by Raven-Hair—Alex. He hadn't forgotten, either, Peter's engaging smile, freckled snub nose and frank blue eyes. They walked on, neither of them attempting to touch the other, in full view as they were of the windows of the backs of the houses in the row where Peter lived, as also from the cliff path that they had just left.

"Before your friend left for the weekend," Peter asked, "did you get as far as fucking with him? Informed by the exhibition Alex and I had given you."

"Not quite," admitted Gary, "although we've progressed to sucking each other's cock. Tom did try to fuck me on Wednesday, but I suddenly started peeing and it put him off, or made him come too quickly, one or the other. Anyway, he ended up shooting off up my back instead."

"You started peeing while he was trying to roger you? That must have made a bit of a mess."

"Well, not that much, actually. I had my trousers down and I was bent over the workbench in the chemistry lab. My prick was actually dangling over the sink, so everything went down the plughole."

Peter smiled. "I wish I could have been a fly on the wall that day. Mind you, mustn't complain. I haven't forgotten you and your friend—Tom?—showing us your handsome cocks. And surprising us by shooting half a mile. That was something to watch."

"Are you planning to have a go at fucking me?" Gary asked, a bit doubtfully.

"We'll see," said Peter. "But I promise I'll do nothing at all that you don't want. Okay?"

They had reached the garden gate. Peter led them in through it, then up the path through a small, rather overgrown, back garden to the kitchen door.

A minute later they were in a small, untidy living room, and Gary was being introduced to Peter's other housemate, the fellow art student who was called Simon. He looked more studious than arty. With medium-length straight dark hair, neatly parted, bashful eyes that peered through neat spectacles, and a neat and tidy nose and mouth, he was undeniably good looking, Gary thought, though in very much a Clark Kent sort of way. He was just finishing a cup of tea. He didn't seem fazed by the idea of Peter coming home with a schoolboy in tow, albeit a fairly mature one. When he'd drained his cup he got to his feet and announced that he was going to the shop to get a few things. Did Peter want anything? Peter said no.

When Simon had gone out Gary asked, "Is he…I mean, does Simon do it with guys?"

"Don't know yet," Peter answered. "He's only been here a fortnight and he's quite shy. He hasn't given any indications, one way or the other. It'd be nice to find he did, though. Especially as he has a cute cock."

"How do you know that," Gary asked, giggling a bit.

"I've seen him wanking. Bit embarrassing, this, but there's a little hole in the wall between his room and the one I share with Alex. Once or twice we've thought he was watching us through it. Just because of a bit of a sound by the wall, that's all. And why not, anyway, if he wants to? But then yesterday when I was on my own and he'd gone upstairs to study—he said—I did just chance to look through the spy hole in the other direction. There he was, on his back on he bed, T-shirt round his armpits and trousers down to his knees, giving himself one. He did it very prettily, I must say, and squirted a big load onto his tummy." Peter looked closely at Gary, an amused grin on his face. "And do you want to know what I did?"

"I guess you may have..." Gary hesitated.

"Wanted to wank. Of course. Everybody who watches another guy doing it wants to do the same thing to himself and does if he gets the chance."

"And yesterday...?" Gary wanted to know.

Peter laughed out loud. "I was too late. I came unexpectedly in my pants before I could get my dick out. Sounds a bit teenage, but there you are. Anyway, now here we are, and Simon won't be back for a while."

Gary thought now that he would have liked to be a fly on the wall, witnessing the scene that Peter had just described. He was titillated by the thought of the serious, bespectacled young man he'd just met boyishly wanking with his trousers at half mast, and of Peter spilling his load while he watched. Now Peter took Gary in his arms. He cuddled him and kissed him and said, "I'd like to fuck you, but only if you want it." He disengaged himself from Gary and sat in an armchair. Gary looked round a bit anxiously. "Don't worry," Peter reassured him, "Simon won't be back for a bit. And if he does come back... Well, you weren't shy of shooting your load in front of me and Alex last weekend, were you?" It struck Gary that Peter had a point. He wouldn't mind much if Simon were to come back and catch them at it. If

Simon enjoyed watching Peter and Alex, let him enjoy the sight of Peter and himself. He had nothing to be bashful about, and decided it might be quite a turn-on to be watched. Peter said, "Sit on my lap," and Gary did.

Expertly Peter slipped Gary's T-shirt up over his head and off, then wriggled his shorts down over his hips. Gary caught Peter's momentary approving smile at the discovery that there was nothing underneath those shorts, save stiff cock and tight balls, nesting in fur. He pulled the shorts right off over Gary's plimsolls, then took those off too, meanwhile keeping Gary firmly planted on his lap, his cock proudly sticking up between his bare thighs like a flagpole.

Gary looked down at himself and approvingly watched the first dewdrop appear from his pee-hole. It felt really nice to sit naked in the lap of someone fully clothed, to feel the warm softness of his sweater against your body, his jeans against your naked young legs. The feel of wool against skin... He remembered how the tickle of the bedcover had caused him to come when, before Tom had taught him to masturbate properly, he had used to brush his cock against it. He wanted to feel that sensation now. He turned himself so that he straddled Peter, facing him, chest to chest, then raised himself a little till he could push his stiff cock against the woolly front of Peter's sweater. On which it promptly deposited a couple of drops of juice.

Peter laughed. "Hey kid, that's nice. That's really sweet. Even if you do end up by making a terrible mess of my pullover."

It was bringing back lovely memories, this tingly feeling of his prick nestling in Peter's woolly clothes, but it wasn't a very comfortable position to sit in for very long. Reluctantly Gary squirmed back round to his original position, sitting across Peter's thighs. He could feel the stirring of Peter's imprisoned cock beneath him. Now he wanted to feel that cock against his skin. Perhaps if Peter's jeans were off, that dick would squeeze its way up between Gary's thighs and stand side by side with Gary's own cock, currently occupying that station on its own. "Take your trousers down," he whispered hotly to Peter. "I want to feel your cock against my bum, between my thighs."

Somehow Peter and Gary together managed to wriggle Peter's jeans down his legs as far as the knees without Gary having to climb off his lap completely. Then Gary squirmed around on top of Peter, feeling his cock move beneath him. Wherever it moved to it anointed him with a drizzle of precome, which Gary enjoyed. One moment it was lined up along the cleft of his bum, the next it had found its way between his thighs and was visible at last, standing to attention right next to Gary's own dick—roundhead next to cavalier—both seeming to compete as to which could dribble juice faster and in the greater quantity. Gary reached down with a finger and ran it round Peter's cock-head gently. Peter did the same to Gary's cock. Both organs quivered in delight.

"This is so good," Gary said, "sitting on you, feeling your cock tickling the inside of my thighs."

"It is," Peter answered. "How would you like it in a slightly different position, just a few inches different, massaging the inside of your inner tube?"

"Inside my arse, you mean?"

"I wasn't going to use such an indelicate expression on this occasion," said Peter, "but I do mean that."

"Yes," said Gary, "I think I would." He gulped. "I'm nervous though. Do you think it'll hurt?"

"Not if I'm careful. And remember, in this position you'll be on top. You'll be the one controlling what happens: how far it goes in and when it comes out. But we have to do something first. And that means getting off me just a moment. Next door in the kitchen there's some olive oil."

Reluctantly, though shivering with excitement, Gary climbed off Peter and fetched the oil from the cupboard in the kitchen where Peter told him to look. (It was easier for him to walk with no clothes on, despite a forward-pointing, dribbling ramrod of an erection, than it was for Peter, whose jeans still tied his legs together at the knees.) When Gary came back Peter made him lie facedown on the sofa for a minute while he opened the oil bottle and poured a little right into Gary's crack. "It's cold," said Gary with a giggle. He felt Gary prize his cheeks apart then felt his finger opening his arse.

"Relax," said Peter, "and let my finger slowly in. Imagine you're sucking a dick and that you're pulling it through your lips." Gary did and it seemed to work. Soon he was aware that Peter's finger had gone in right to the hilt, and was wiping his insides all round with oil. Gently, slowly Peter pulled his finger out. Gary's arse, where it had been, felt hot, almost like burning, but not unpleasantly so. Then he realized that the sensation was not merely pleasant, it was a wonder, and he wanted it to go on—he wanted Peter's cock inside him now.

Peter sat down again on the sofa, poured a drop of oil down onto his prick and worked it round the head and shaft with his hand. "Now sit on my lap like you did before, and this time wriggle your oily little orifice round over the head of my dick and let it slip in."

Gingerly, Gary lowered himself toward Peter's lap, feeling his way toward his cock with his bum (a novel experience for him—but then, what wasn't a novel experience today?) He felt the hard cock-tip prod against first one cheek and then the other, then somehow it had found its way into the cleft between. "Imagine you're going to swallow it with your hole," Peter reminded him.

Then suddenly, without warning, Peter's cock had gone in. Gary found himself sliding down it slowly, like a slow-motion fireman down a pole. He felt himself flooded with radiance, with heat, with sensation. Peter had somehow got right into his insides.

Gary realized that he was sitting firmly on Peter's lap now. All of Peter's prick was poking up his arse. There was no more to take unless he were to try to swallow his balls. Peter spoke. "I might just come without anything more happening, but it'll be nice for both of us if you move yourself up and down. Not too far though, or with all this oil my dick'll slip out."

Their attention was suddenly caught by a movement by the door. They turned their heads, though nothing else. There in the doorway stood Simon, mouth agape with astonishment and shock, a state soon mirrored by Peter and Gary. They sat frozen where they were, their mouths too dropping open in surprise, though their pricks stayed stiff—Gary could see his own, and he felt the comfort and solidity of Peter's thick shaft, upright in his arse. Then, very slowly, Simon's expression thawed into a grin, as he began to unbuckle the belt of his jeans and undo the studs of his fly. "Just keep on going," Simon said, "if you're okay with an audience."

Gary confirmed just then what he had suspected: that having an audience was absolutely fine. And if that audience was going to take its trousers down and show its appreciation by pleasuring itself while it watched, that was just fine too. Gary started to do what naturally seemed to be required. His feet weren't touching the ground now so he couldn't use them for leverage. Instead he used his arms, which he'd thrown around Peter's neck in a sort of ecstasy, to pull his body up a bit. With that and some wriggling of his thighs and bum he somehow managed to massage Peter's cock, thick and fleshy inside him, up and down. "Something tells me this isn't going to take long," Peter said, directing the remark toward Simon, and grasped Gary's cock with his own, oil-lubricated, hand.

Simon, meanwhile, still standing in the doorway, had slipped his jeans all the way down his legs, produced a rapidly stiffening uncircumcised dick that was as handsome as the rest of him, in the same modest way. He had nice strong legs, well shaped, and, because his T-shirt was very short, he was exposing his belly too. It was striated with fine hair that ran in elegant waves from his central treasure trail as neatly as if parted with a comb. Grinning silently, Simon proceeded to wank himself unhurriedly off, bending slightly at the knees as he approached his climax, and finally spilling big white gobbets of come onto the carpet in front of his feet.

"Oh, wow, that looked so good," Gary said. He felt he was in heaven now. Looking down at his own cock, he could see that Peter moving his hand—with his exertions, Gary was having his own little fuck in the cozy, slithery warmth of Peter's fist.

"I'm coming," Peter announced. "You won't be surprised."

"Me too," said Gary, "and no surprise there either. Oh hey, here I go!" He felt his spunk rising inside him and it made him redouble his attempts to move up and down in Peter's lap and in Peter's fist. With total abandon, he shot his load, at exactly the same moment as Peter gasped and shot his too, hot and copious into Gary. There was no high-thrown plume from Gary's cock this time—the sight that Peter might have been hoping for, though Peter was shooting his own load with such joyous abandon at that moment that he was hardly going to care. With all his convulsions, thrustings and writhing of his body, Gary's spunk flew out of him spinning in all directions, as if through a fast revolving fan or helicopter-blades. At the same time he felt Peter's hot pumping inside him—it seemed that Peter was pumping his sperm spurts forever.

But then at last their frantic movements slowed; the tempest of delight that had sprung up and raged in both of them died down. While Simon continued to watch them, still gently fondling his slick, spent but still stiff prick, Peter slid his cock out of Gary and allowed him to climb off his lap. Peter stood up. "Come here," he said to Simon, and without bothering to pull up their jeans they shuffled toward each other across the carpet. Of the three of them only Gary was completely undressed, but that was clearly not going to remain the case for long. "I think the three of us ought to get up to the bedroom now," Peter said. He slid Simon's T-shirt up and off over his head, then Simon did the same to him. As they came close together so their upslanting dicks came together too, and their two foreskins kissed each other gently like little lips.

Standing naked, watching, just a few feet away, Gary ran a finger gently along the underside ridge of his own stiff organ, as if checking that he was awake and that this was not all a dream.

What a lot he would be able to tell Tom when he got back to school...

IN THE CLOSET

Michael Bracken

When I heard the apartment door open I stopped cold. Christopher Melon had returned home earlier than usual, and the sound of two male voices entering the apartment told me he wasn't alone. I stood in his master bedroom dressed all in black, a thick wad of his cash in one pocket, several expensive pieces of his jewelry in another.

The apartment had two exits—the door from the hallway through which Christopher and his guest had entered and the sliding glass door leading to the balcony through which I had entered twenty minutes earlier. The only path to either exit was through the living room where, from the sound of things, Christopher was preparing drinks at the wet bar.

My pulse raced and I struggled to keep my breathing steady. I had never before been trapped in a residence I was burglarizing. The closest I had ever come was more than a decade earlier, when I'd been younger and less cautious. I'd slipped out the back door of a Tudor in the Heights just as the homeowners entered through the front.

I ventured a glance into the living room. Slim, dishwater-blond, impeccably groomed Christopher stood with his back to me. His guest, a slightly older, dark-haired man with broad shoulders and thick arms barely contained by the sleeves of his Polo shirt, stood staring into Christopher's eyes. Both held drinks.

Christopher was a regular at the Cock and Bull, one of several establishments I frequented in search of appropriate marks, but his guest was unfamiliar. When the older man wet his lips with the tip of his tongue and ran the backs of his fingers down Christopher's cheek, I knew I didn't have much time. Christopher immediately placed his unfinished drink on an end table, took his guest's hand and turned in my direction. As they approached the bedroom I backed away from the door and slipped into the walk-in closet. I left the door open a fraction of an inch so I could peek through the crack and see what was happening.

The two men didn't waste any time. They barely made it into the bedroom before the bigger man pushed Christopher against the wall only inches from the closet door. He covered Christopher's mouth with his, and one hand groped the smaller man's crotch. Christopher's slender hands fumbled with the bigger man's belt, button and zipper and soon freed his long, thick-shafted erection.

They spun around so that the dark-haired man's back was against the wall and Christopher dropped to his knees on the carpet before him. He wrapped both hands around the thick cock jutting in front of his face and took the spongy soft mushroom cap into his mouth. He licked, he sucked and then he drew in another inch of the bigger man's shaft.

That wasn't enough for the bigger man. He grabbed the back of Christopher's head and thrust his hips forward, sinking the entire length of his cock into Christopher's oral cavity. I expected

Christopher to gag, but he didn't, unexpectedly impressing me. Then the bigger man drew his hips back until just his cockhead remained in Christopher's mouth before he pushed forward again. His heavy ball sac bounced off Christopher's chin, and he did it again and again.

As I watched the dark-haired man face-fuck Christopher so close to me I could have reached out of the closet and touched them, my cock began to thicken and rise. I carefully shifted position to untangle it from my briefs.

The bigger man's hips began pumping faster and then he suddenly stopped with his cock buried deep inside Christopher's mouth. I watched Christopher's Adam's apple bob up and down as he swallowed wad after wad of the bigger man's cum, and I swallowed hard, too, because I almost came in my shorts.

When Christopher finally pulled away, a thin string of cum stretched from his lips to the bigger man's rapidly deflating cock until it finally snapped as Christopher stood.

The two men stepped away from the wall and out of my line of sight until I realized I could see the entire bedroom reflected in the mirror hung above the dresser. I watched as they stripped off their clothes. Christopher had the light, all-over tan of someone who spent time in a tanning booth. Though his face, neck and arms were the leather-brown of someone who spent a lot of time outdoors, Christopher's guest was eggshell white beneath his clothes, his only color provided by a light dusting of black body hair.

By the time they finished removing their clothes, the dark-haired man's cock had begun to resume its former stature. Christopher reached into his nightstand and retrieved a partially used tube of lube. He handed it to his guest and then lay back on the bed. His guest lay beside him and opened the tube. After he slathered lube between Christopher's asscheeks and on his own thick cock, he lifted the slender blond's legs and nearly folded Christopher in half. Then he pressed his cockhead against Christopher's lube-slathered sphincter and pressed forward until he buried his cock deep inside Christopher's ass.

Christopher's cock was trapped between them and, as the bigger man drew back and pressed forward, his abdomen rubbed against the underside of Christopher's stiff shaft.

Christopher came first, covering them with his sticky effluent. Then his guest made one final deep thrust and he came, emptying himself within Christopher.

I was so excited I felt my underwear dampen with precum, and it took tremendous willpower not to pull my cock out and stroke it into submission. I didn't dare though. I knew that getting caught in a man's closet with his valuables in my pockets was bad, but getting caught in his closet with my hand wrapped around my valuables was infinitely worse. So, my erection and I waited patiently while the two men snuggled, fucked yet again and then snuggled more.

I waited a long time in that closet, until I was certain, from the sound of their breathing, that both men were asleep. Then I slipped from the bedroom, across the living room, out through the sliding glass door, and over the rail to the ground one floor below. My nondescript car, parked two blocks away, remained undisturbed.

Once home, I sat on the toilet, took my still-hard cock in my hand, and churned butter until I came with a rush that painted the back of the bathroom door with cum before I could catch it in the tissue I held in my free hand.

The next day I fenced Christopher's jewelry, more valuable for its gold content than its craftsmanship, and pocketed the cash. That evening I took myself out for a steak dinner accompanied by a moderately priced bottle of wine and flirted with my handsome waiter. Tony had waited on me several times over the years I'd been dining at Carvello's but was half of a committed relationship and had long ago made it clear that nothing would ever come of my flirtation.

Then I relaxed that evening at Leon's, a dark neighborhood bar where I could enjoy myself without thinking about work. Other evenings in other bars led to other apartments and other homes. As nondescript as my car, I watched the pickups and kiss-offs, learning the routines of potential marks. I paid attention to who went home early and who remained until closing, who left alone and who left on the arm of another man, and who actually had money and who merely fronted. I followed the best marks, learned where they lived, and determined whose homes were easily accessible and whose were best avoided. Then, when I felt confident that I would have sufficient uninterrupted time, I visited some of those homes, leaving with hundreds and sometimes thousands of dollars worth of cash and easily fenced valuables.

And every time I was inside one of those homes without an invitation, I thought about what I'd seen in Christopher Melon's apartment. I'd never thought of myself as the type of guy who liked to watch other men having sex—I hadn't even watched porn since dropping out of junior college—but I frequently found myself churning butter while mentally replaying that scene.

I worked a circuit, never too many consecutive nights spent at the same bar, never at the same bar so often that bartenders and barflies recognized me, but often enough that I knew the routines of their most affluent regulars. Then one night I found myself back at the Cock and Bull, Christopher Melon's favorite watering hole, and he was there, leaning against the bar, waiting to be approached. My cock twitched at the memory of

Christopher giving his dark-haired guest a blow job only inches from me.

I plied Christopher with drinks, maybe even using his own money, and soon felt his hand between my thighs, cupping my balls and squeezing my tumescent cock through the material of my chinos. I already knew what he looked like naked, what he looked like with a cock in his mouth, and what he looked like in the throes of passion. What I didn't know, until that moment, is what he felt like, and I liked the way my cock felt in his hand, even with layers of cloth between them. I watched his reflection in the mirror behind the bar, much like I had watched his reflection that night in his bedroom, and I suggested there might be somewhere private we could go.

Christopher removed his hand from my crotch, finished his drink and took me back to his apartment. Once inside he offered me a drink, apparently following some long-established script of seduction.

I declined the drink, took his hand and led him to his bedroom.

"You act like you've been here before," he said.

I didn't say anything. Instead, I opened the closet door and looked inside.

"What are you doing?" he asked.

"Humor me," I said. "This will just take a moment."

I enjoyed watching but I wouldn't enjoy being watched. I switched on the light, saw nothing but clothing and shoes, and switched it off again.

Then I turned to Christopher, pulled him into my arms, and covered his mouth with mine. We kissed long, deep and hard before I peeled off his clothes and fucked him until he screamed with pleasure.

HAREM

Jeff Mann

Gawking. It's undignified and a little pathetic, but I can't help myself. Outside, rangy Conrad, the arborist, directs his crew of compatriots. Inside, I stand by the window, longing.

They're taking down dead branches over the driveway. One worker's in an elevated bucket three stories off the ground, brandishing a chainsaw. Conrad paces on my back deck, giving orders. It's a cool October day. He's dressed in a Virginia Tech baseball cap, a sweatshirt, jeans, and work boots, but I'm trying to visualize him in nothing but briefs. I'd kill to see the guy stripped down. As it is, there's a rip in the seat of his pants—seems almost deliberately placed, as if he knows I want him—that reveals teasing flashes of white underwear.

Like most men, I've done this all my adult life: peering surreptitiously at someone I'd fuck in a heartbeat given a more conducive state of affairs. When it comes to erotic satisfaction, my circumstances have rarely been ideal. I'm not gorgeous, not charming, never have been. I've always been shy, insecure, for the most part incapable of making a pass. I grew up in and have chosen to remain in the Highland South, where many homophobes and conservatives lurk, where there is relatively little gay life or queer-friendly spaces. Finally, I've always been attracted to butch men and country boys, meaning the objects of my lust are most likely straight and thus not approachable.

And now middle age has become a handicap. I'm chunky, with a graying beard. I shave my head, the only dignified response to male pattern baldness. Yeah, I'm fairly handsome for fifty-two, if I may say so myself, and I'm lifting heavier weights than I ever have in my life, meaning that my chest, shoulders, and arms are pretty impressive for a man my age, and, thanks to the stationary bike, I still possess a decently defined set of hairy legs. But let's just say that I am acutely aware of erotic possibility drying up, and that slow recession makes me frantic, the "quiet desperation" Thoreau spoke of. Like anyone with a libido, I want to be desirable so as to successfully attract the desirable, but the seasons come and go, faster and faster, it seems, and I can imagine with ease a day not too far distant when I've lost whatever appeal I have left. Doug, my partner, he's vanilla, while I'm compulsively kinky, a rabid fan of ropes, gags and rough sex, plus we've been together for fifteen years, meaning by now we're more comfortable companions than lovers, and so my erotic interest is more and more directed elsewhere.

Elsewhere today is Conrad. After so many decades of studying good-looking men, up close and from a distance, I'm an expert at calculating what a clothed man might look like naked. I'm good at gauging, despite the concealment of garments, a guy's musculature, cock size, and body hair. Conrad's very lean, that's obvious. My guess is that his chest is lightly muscled, very pale, with light hair rimming small nipples. His cock's big, like most tall, wiry men. His butt's tight, white and curved just right, with abundant golden fur in the crack. His legs are coated with hair just as golden.

Distance and secrecy—hiding behind cracked blinds or barely parted drapes—give peepers like me the advantage of staring at prey without being noticed. Believe me, most guys I furtively admire in this little mountain town would passionately, even violently, object to an openly lecherous stare from another man. Not only do I not want to end up in a fistfight, I don't want to give offense. I was raised with good manners. I don't want men like Conrad to feel uncomfortable or insulted or regard me as an old lech or pervert. So I ogle them from the shadows.

But there's something to be said for proximity. Near them, I can't stare freely, but I can interact with them, listen to their deep voices and country accents, even get a faint whiff of their bodies. So now I step outside.

"Howdy," says Conrad, smiling. He's about thirty, with pale-blue eyes, a thin face, high cheekbones and a prominent Adam's apple. His chin and cheeks are coated with a tasty layer of blond beard-stubble. Curly blond hair covers his lean forearms. Sun glints off his wedding ring.

"Uh, uh, we're about done. You want those hemlocks treated while we're here? And, uh, we could dust that crabapple with lime."

We confer. I want to hug him, to pull his sweatshirt up to see if there's any hair on his belly. When he bends to brush sawdust off a boot, the sweatshirt rides up in back just far enough to give me a glimpse of his briefs' waistband, and above that, a strip of skin.

I get tired of being a human being in a world of law. Don't you? I want to growl like a hungry wolf, grab Conrad by the shoulders, push him back against the wall and kiss him hard. I want to feel his beard-stubble against my face.

* * *

Doug's up at daybreak. He heads down the hall to his home office to work. I lie here, groggy, the tabbies sprawled at my feet. I stroke myself into hardness, then reach for a Kleenex.

Conrad struggles beneath me as I bind him, but his resistance only excites me more. Soon, I have his sinewy nakedness trussed so tightly he can do little more than flop around like a landed trout. Silvery strips of duct tape secure his arms and wrists behind him; his knees and ankles are similarly restrained.

"Let me loose, man! Please!" Conrad pants.

"Shhh," I say, cutting another long strip of tape off the roll with my army knife. I press the tape over Conrad's mouth, wrapping it around his head till he's silenced with three layers' worth. "You need to keep very still now."

Conrad lies there, trembling, as I trail the blade's sharp point over his hard nipples, along the slight curves of his pecs, down along his flat abs, along a prominent hip bone and into the blond shrubby tangles of his pubes. When I run the edge over his soft cock, it hardens.

"You like this, huh?" I say, stroking his stiffening length with steel.

Conrad whimpers. He blinks his blue eyes. A tear rolls down his right cheek. He shakes his head.

I keep stroking the shaft. He shudders and grows harder still.

"Tell the truth," I say, placing the tip of the knife against his glans. A few drops of precum have collected there. I wipe them up with the knifepoint and lick the juice off the steel. "You don't like this, do you? You love it."

Conrad nods. Another tear courses down his cheek, then another and another.

"Beauty broken down. God, I love it when you cry," I say,

stroking the knife along his prick again. Halfway through my fifth excursion from cock-base to cock-tip, Conrad goes taut and releases a strained sob. Wet eyes clenched shut, he cums.

The boy's short and lean, in filthy jeans. Hard muscles line his tanned, tattooed arms; his chest swells beneath a dirty white tank top. His hair's wavy and golden-brown, the color of his close-cut goatee. He's probably in his late twenties and looks country as they come. I move from window to window like a cat would following a hopping robin, watching as the guy works. He climbs up and down the ladder, balances along a scaffold, shoulders packs of roof tiles, and pushes a wheelbarrow of debris across the lawn to his truck. I should be writing; I should be reading. I can't. I'm transfixed. I won't be able to concentrate on anything else until the day is done and the guy leaves with his fellow roofers.

The new roof comes with a lifetime warranty. Six thousand dollars, not bad for such a big job. Chalk the reasonable price up to living in southwest Virginia, where the cost of living is low, the mountain landscape beautiful and religious fundamentalists plentiful as fleas on a street-cur. Certainly there are no leather bars around where I might meet a perverse, submissive version of my little roofer, some savory cub aching to spend an afternoon ball-gagged and hog-tied on the floor of his Daddy-bear's closet.

Today's another day I'll have to forego sex and settle for scenery. Right now Roofer-Cub's taking a lunch break beneath the Norway maple in the front lawn, while I stand in the shadows of my study, squeezing my crotch, memorizing him for later. He leans back against the trunk, chewing a sandwich and enjoying the shade; he smokes a cigarette and chats on his cell phone, probably to his wife or girlfriend, some lucky buxom blonde who's likely to bear him several children. In ten years they'll be living in a trailer, she'll be fat-slabbed, the children will be shrill and frenetic and he'll be gaunt, irritable and aging fast.

I see my opportunity for closer inspection when, done with lunch, he gets out an odd implement and starts rolling it over the lawn. When my cock's softened sufficiently not to be an obscene projection in my cargo shorts, I step outside onto the stoop.

"Howdy," I say. So many pretexts I've composed over the years, just to get nearer to delectable strangers. Today's is simple: putting a letter in the mailbox.

"Hey, buddy. How you?" The cub looks my way and smiles.

I glance up at the pitched roof. "Tiles are looking great." I grew up around here, patterning my version of manhood on the rural and blue-collar types I grew up around. I can make redneck small talk with the best of them.

I extend a hand. "I'm Jeff."

He wipes his hand on his pants. "Kinda dirty, bud. Sorry. Name's Luke." We shake firmly, skin pressed to skin—two lives, two strengths briefly aligned.

Our hands part. I resist the urge to pull him into my arms. I'll probably never get to touch him again. "So what's that thang there you're using?"

"It's a roller magnet, buddy. See here?" He runs it across the lawn. "It's a'pickin' up nails and tacks from the grass."

Luke has the kind of voice that always turns me on: low, casual, with thick country vowels, what I used to call "uneducated Southern" before Doug pointed out to me that I sound much the same when I'm drunk, pissed off, horny or high, or when I'm around other small-town Southerners.

"Cool," I say, moving closer, doing my best to veil my hungry fascination. I'd give anything for a whiff of his armpits. They have to be ripe, after hours working in the warm May sun. It's all about the senses, isn't it? The more stimulated, the better. Sight's been feasting all morning, hearing's just been titillated, now smell wants something to savor. Taste and touch, they're snarling with frustration, aching to finger the small buds of those nipples, tiny protuberances beneath his tight tank top, to lap that gleam of sweat on his clavicles, to nuzzle the musky dark between his buttcheeks. Small and compact as he is, I could lift him into my arms and carry him into the house. I doubt that such an enthusiastic gesture would be welcomed.

"Where'd you get the ink? I got this done in Blacksburg." I lift a tattoo-sleeved arm.

"That's a lotta fine work. Me," Luke says, flexing veiny brown biceps, "I got all this in Harlan. Kentucky, y'know. Worked as a miner for a while."

In an ideal world, I'd offer him a beer and a blow job. Instead I say, "My best friend in college was the son of a miner. Damned hard work."

"Buddy, don't you know it! There I was, a'diggin' deep in the earth, and now I'm high in the sky. Risking my ass either way. But a man's gotta work, right?"

"Well, I better let you get back to it," I say. I can't sustain these little chats for long. Between my innate shyness and the struggle to appear not ravenous but calm, they sap me of energy fast. "Sure, buddy," he says with a nod, returning his attentions to the lawn.

I go inside, back into my rapt shadow-cloaked study of him. When he leaves the front yard, I pad through the house, checking each window, tracking him like a hunter would a deer. I find him on the roof scaffolding again, just outside the small window of the upstairs laundry room. Good god, he's taken his tank top off. There are more tattoos on his chest and belly; his torso's covered with sweat and a dusting of golden-brown fur; his nipples are tiny, brown and erect; and there's a scar on his back, a shiny swelling where a serious injury might have been, perhaps even a gunshot wound.

I step back, where I can still see Luke but he can't see me. I pore over the lines and colors of his exposed torso; I grip the cloth covering my cock and squeeze. I keep squeezing. Before a minute's out, I've shot a big load into my boxer briefs. "Thanks, buddy," I whisper. Chuckling, I head into the bathroom to clean myself up.

The roofers leave at four. I'm relieved. Finally I can concentrate on something else. I catch up on email, then make notes for an essay I plan to write tomorrow. Later I'll make Doug and me martinis and throw together some dinner; right now I'm going to do my best to retain the "muscle" in "muscle-bear" by lifting weights in the basement gym.

My "Macho Room," I call it. There are several posters of muscled, half-naked guys; a stationary bike; a television on which to watch porn while I pedal; racks of free weights; a punching bag; and a bench press, with a barbell in the stand at its head and an inclined pad for preacher curls at its foot. Listening to country music, I work through biceps, then deltoids, then biceps again, finishing with triceps. A long shower next, since my husbear is always complaining about my strong body odor. I think I smell sexy and butch; he thinks I stink.

Water runs down my body; it feels like hands stroking me. I close my eyes, think of my little roofer and get hard again. Why can't it be him touching me, our bodies pressed together in the shower? Why can't I find a part-time boy who looks like that? The world's so fucking unaccommodating. Absentmindly, I tug on myself for a few frustrated seconds before drying off.

Luke's groaning with discomfort when I step out of the shower. He's stripped, bent over, tied belly-down to the preacher-curl bench. His arms are spread, tautly stretched out, wrists roped to the heavy barbell resting in the stand before him. His head's bowed; a ball-gag's strapped between his teeth; drool drips from his mouth, spattering the black bench press.

"Want loose yet?" I say. I run a hand down his tanned back, then over the white mounds of his ass. "It's been two hours. You've got to be sore."

"Uhhmm-huh." The boy lifts his head and nods, then elevates his butt, pressing it against my palm.

"Want to be fucked first, huh? I hope so, 'cause it's happening whether you want it to or not."

I slip a finger between his buttocks. Here's his moist hole, at the bottom of this shallow valley forested with fur. When I nudge it, Luke groans and cocks his rear higher.

"How about some torture to warm you up? Think you can endure a little pain for Daddy?"

His nod's pure eagerness.

I snap a leather parachute around the base of his balls, then hang a work boot from it. I slip weighted clamps on his nipples. I take a riding crop to his back and shoulders, then to the snowy curves of his ass, then to his upper thighs. He squirms and whines, yanking hard on his bonds, then, as the blows get harder, thrashes and shouts. The weights hanging from his tits and ball sac sway and jolt. His slobber puddles on the bench. His strained screams shatter, melting into sobs. Soon, tears join his pooled drool.

Nothing moves me like manly helplessness and manly tears. I stop beating Luke only after I've covered him with red welts from his shoulders to the back of his knees. He lies heaving across the tilted pad. "Good, good boy," I say, dropping the crop. "You took a lot." Kneeling, I spread his blow-heated, crimson-etched buttocks and give his hole a long tonguing. He quivers and slumps; he whimpers and moans.

Now I stand. I lube us up. I finger him, stretching him open. When I push my cockhead up his ass, he jerks, tugs on his wrist-ropes, and whines with pain.

"God, you're tight. Feels great." I edge in a mite deeper. His channel's narrow resistance is making my balls throb.

"Ever had a man's dick up your butt before?"

Luke winces. He shakes his head. His bound hands claw air, then clench.

"Does it hurt?" I slide in an inch deeper still.

Luke nods.

"Too bad. You'll get used to it." I pull out, rub my cockhead up and down his crack and then shove all the way inside. Luke howls. I wrap an arm around his tight torso, press a hand over his mouth, and spear him hard. One minute he's struggling, shaking his head frantically, begging me to stop; the next, I'm jacking him, he's bucking back against me, then prick-pounding my fist; and the next, I'm cumming up his ass and he's cumming in my hand.

"Jeff, you might want to get up here," Doug says softly from the head of the stairs. "I don't think you want to miss this."

Outside, a gray-grim day in mid-December, another set of workers moves up and down ladders set against the front of the house. Last year was the roof; this year we're having storm windows installed before winter sets in. As usual, I'm mesmerized by a member of the work crew. Once again he's younger and smaller than I—in his midtwenties, about five-nine—contrasts that bring out the BDSM Top in me, the doting, stern/tender Daddy. He sports wavy brown hair and a close-trimmed dark goatee. His sweatshirts have been close-fitting enough to let me know his chest, shoulders and arms are solid and muscular. Talk about eminently fuckable. He's very handsome, resembling a younger version of Tim McGraw, my favorite country music star. In the couple of days the guy's been working here, Doug and I have nicknamed him "Baby Tim."

"It's your new *boy*friend." Doug's voice is a mocking sing-song. "Best view yet."

I take the steps two at a time, which is more difficult than it used to be. When I enter Doug's office, my quarry's atop a ladder right outside the window.

"Watch now," says Doug. "When he stretches up to put the new window frame in."

As much as I want to stare openly, I don't. Doug and I pretend to be engrossed with something on his computer monitor.

"There. Look," Doug whispers.

Trying to seem casual, I lift my head. When Baby Tim lifts the window frame, his sweatshirt rides up. For a precious handful of seconds, I can see the top of his loins' lean lyre and a brown line of belly hair leading into his jeans.

"Oh, fuck!" I gasp. I put on an elaborate show of false focus, pointing at something supposedly significant on the monitor, meanwhile watching like a raptor out of the corner of my eye. Once again, the brief stretching; once again, the sweet exposure of Baby Tim's furry belly. Storm windows are supposed to be about keeping the warmth in and the cold out, but right now it feels like the opposite. I'm the chilly one, separated from all that hairy heat by a pane of glass, a titanium wall of social custom, heteronormativity, several decades and my own cowardice.

Doug's out of town, so I play the soundtrack to *Thor* extra loud. It's flurrying outside; my study's dark except for the light of one candle. I'm sipping a peaty Irish whiskey, one boot propped up on my handsome human footstool.

Baby Tim's naked, on his hands and knees. His wrists are roped together in front of him. A leather dog collar and leash are buckled around his neck; there's a butt plug up his ass and a camo bandana knotted between his teeth. He grunts, shifts his hips then settles back into acquiescent stillness.

I finish my drink, lift my boot off the small of his back and rise. "Good meal you cooked tonight, cub. You ready for bed?"

He nods. Bending, I work the plug around. When I pull it out, Tim whines with disappointment.

"Don't worry, boy, I have something larger that's going up your ass real soon." Taking the leash, I lead him upstairs, where we can enjoy the gas fireplace. I strip, then push him onto the bed, tie his wrists to the headboard, position him on his elbows and knees and enter him roughly from behind. His butt's small, very tight and coated with dark hair.

"Like this?" I say, pounding him vigorously.

"Ooo yah! Ooooo yah!" he shouts. His words may be muffled by cloth but his ardor's more than clear.

"On your back now?"

"Yah, yah!" He nods wildly.

I pull out, roll him over, bend him double, and plunge in again. "Want it harder?"

"Yah!" Tim growls. His ankles lock behind my back, pulling me more deeply into him. I've only managed a dozen thrusts when he goes taut and gasps. His untouched cock spurts, jetting onto my chin and pulsing over his hairy belly.

Chuckling, I rub cum into my beard and lick up the pool on his stomach before pulling out and untying him. "I'm tired, cub," I say, folding him into my arms, fondling his nipples.

"Let's just cuddle. I don't need to cum right now. I'll plow you again in the morning. Would you like that?"

"Uhhhhhh huh!" Baby Tim nods, nuzzles his gagged mouth against my chest and scoots closer. Tomorrow morning, I'll teach my new houseboy to make buckwheat pancakes. After breakfast, he'll spend a few happy hours hog-tied in the closet.

The dick-dancer gyrating before me began in a skimpy pair of underwear on the big center stage, but now he's naked, on a brightly lit dais only yards away. Unlike the other performers, he's not gym-chiseled. His body is simply a young man's: lean, with muscle-thick, hairy thighs and some slight definition in the shoulders and chest. His dick isn't particularly big, and he isn't much of a dancer. He pretty much just moves his hips forward and back, flopping his soft cock around. But for some reason I can't explain, I'm attracted almost invariably to Caucasians, and he's one of the few white guys dancing. I dote on facial hair and body hair, and he's got a chinstrap beard and the slightest dusting of fur on his torso, while all his fellow dancers are clean shaven and smooth chested. Finally, his pale body is scattered with tattoos, which are always an erotic addition, and he's wearing black harness-strap boots exactly like a pair I own, making him look like a country boy.

It's late, and I'm tired. I only came here to please Doug, who relishes such venues. Strip clubs always make me uncomfortable. I feel old, ugly, frustrated, like a supplicant. The contrast between middle-aged patrons and young, well-built dancers is painful, really. I don't want to want men I can't have. I don't want to stare lustfully at someone I can't fuck, someone who feels my need, finds such need pathetic, yet revels in the ego-food my attentions provide. If I'm going to ogle, I want to ogle while unseen. I don't want someone to smile at me and flirt with me only because I might give him money. It's humiliating, one-sided. My desire makes me feel weak, not powerful; ashamed, not proud.

But, minute by minute, this dancer's winning me over with his limber body and shaggy brown hair. His face is only vaguely handsome, almost coarse, but when he smiles, his features transform: he glows, he's endearing. He's a gay farm-boy come to the big city, I tell myself, making a living as best he can, relishing his new life in the nation's teeming capital but still homesick for Southern hills and fields. If only he found the right Daddy to take care of him. This guy's the most delicious fuel for fantasy I've encountered in months.

Doug's amused by my interest. He rises—as I definitely cannot, thoroughly paralyzed as I am by my own sheepish desire—steps over to the dancer, whispers to him and slips bills inside the high socks the boy's wearing beneath his boots. The dancer nods, flashes me that amazing smile and turns his back to us.

"I told him you were an ass man," Doug says, grinning.

The dancer bends over, cocks his rear-end in my direction, wriggles it then slaps his right buttcheek hard. He drops to his hands and knees, still swaying to the music. Light gleams on the bunched muscles of his shoulders, the dip of his spine, the lift of his buttocks. He's presenting his ass to me like a gift. I can see, as clearly as any beauty I've ever adored, fine hairs like gold thread covering the pale mounds of his buttocks.

Dizzy, almost stunned, I sit back. I gulp my gin and tonic, feigning an exterior of cool dignity, but inside I'm feeling like one of those cartoon characters whose eyes bug out a foot and whose jaw drops to the ground like an anvil. The boy slaps his left buttock now, looks back at me and grins, then pulls the mound of flesh aside, far enough for me to see his cleft's copper hair and his asshole. The tiny aperture clenches and relaxes. "I think he's winking at you," Doug says in my ear.

I am, simply put, enflamed. Dry mouth, beating heart. I might as well be a love-struck adolescent. For once, I give over my shame and pride and simply wallow flush-cheeked inside infatuation, gawking at those two low hills, the mossy vale between them, and the tight delight waiting there. That a man might give me such a show, offer me such blessings, and then leave me unsated is simply unthinkable. Obscene, really. What's right is that I stand up, stride over, beat his ass scarlet and then plow him in front of this room of strangers.

Too soon the besotting butt-show's done. He stands, turns around, gives me another white smile, fingers his nipples a little, which only maddens me more, and then the song's ended. He hops off the dais, lopes over and drops to his knees before us. "Hey, I'm Byron," he says, placing one hand on my knee, the other on Doug's.

We chat; I do my best not to stutter, not to pounce on him. He's from Alexandria, just finished college in North Carolina. We have matching tattoos: daggers on our left forearms. He seems innocent, cheerful, friendly, polite. I wonder how much of him is façade, meant to win more bills from us. I don't beg him to go home with us. I don't ask him if more money might buy a lengthier, more intimate show back in our hotel room.

Too soon, the naked boy kneeling at my feet rises. "Real nice meeting you all," he says. With a smile, he disappears into the crowd.

It's after midnight; Doug and I have to drive home early tomorrow. But we stay; I want more of Byron. In a little bit he's back, this time dancing on top of the bar. He locks one leg around a ceiling pipe, swinging nimbly from it like a tattooed Tarzan. He talks with a hideous Asian man who's clearly as smitten with him as I am. I feel jealous, absurdly possessive. "Get away from him, you troll! That's my boy!" I want to shout.

Instead, as soon as said troll strolls on, I gather my courage, walk over and slip a bill into Byron's sock. He grins down at me, his penis flopping mere inches from my face. All I'd need to do is open my mouth and lean forward, and his cock would be pulsing between my lips. I could fondle him—prominent signs around the club make clear that you can touch a dancer below the knees and above the navel. I could run my fingers over his hairy calves, stroke his mouthwatering nipples, caress his armpit hair. I want to touch him as much as I've wanted anything. But why madden myself more? Why open the floodgates further? Instead I ask him about several of his tattoos, slip another bill inside his sock, say, "Thanks for the great show. Really amazing," and head back through the crowd to my gin and tonic. As soon as the song ends and Byron descends, Doug and I depart.

Daddybear's harem, I wryly call them, the men my memory's collected, the ones I make love to in my mind. I plug them into a simple erotic equation (scruffy butch man + bondage + gags + torture + ass-rape) that never fails to stoke me up and get me off. Now it's time for Byron to take his turn.

It's a windy evening; I spend hours reading. I look up from my book often to admire my guest, who's lying naked before the fireplace. He's silent except for an occasional discomfited grunt as he shifts about on the carpet. Every now and then, our eyes meet and hold. Every now and then, his limbs strain, a struggle as brief as it is futile, before, defeated, he bows his head, sighs and surrenders.

The gas fire has the bedroom snug, so my captive's suffering isn't about temperature but about the wicked ingenuity of his restraint. His hands, tied behind his back, are anchored with a short cord to his trussed-up cock and balls, meaning that every time he fights his bonds, he only tortures his own genitals. His hairy legs are bent behind him, his ankles crossed, tied, and tethered to the wooden dowel roped between his teeth, so that any half-hearted attempts at escape only wedge the stick deeper into his mouth. Byron's been squirming and groaning for a good three hours, giving me a show so beautiful that my book's gotten only intermittent attention. But now this chapter's done, and I think Byron's had enough.

Bending, I stroke his shaggy hair and then free him, leaving only the dowel-gag in place. With difficulty he crawls to his knees, limbs clearly sore from long hours of constriction. Gratefully, he wraps his arms around my waist and presses his face against my belly.

"Show me your hole," I say, squeezing his shoulders. "Like you did before." Compliant, he crawls over to the bed, bends over the edge, reaches back with both hands, and spreads his asscheeks.

"Good boy. Keep yourself spread. Stay just like that." I take a deep breath before stripping off my clothes and dropping to my knees behind him. I push my face into that fine copper crevice-fur, breathing in his musk, probing him with my tongue-tip, adoring the glossy pink entrance there. I rim him tirelessly, relishing his ecstatic moans, the way he wriggles his butt against my beard.

"Time for the cuffs," I say, seizing Byron's wrists and locking them behind his back. I lube us up and jam in overlapped fingers, prying him open further. Finally, I poke my cockhead between his buttocks and thrust inside, making him wince and yelp. I grip his hips and fuck him with snarling brutality. The bed creaks, bumping against the wall.

"How's this, you little tease?" I growl, swatting his

buttcheeks. "Isn't this what you were begging for? About time that gorgeous ass of yours got filled up."

Byron moans and nods. I pound him mercilessly, till he's whimpering with pain. Expertly, his ass-canal clenches and pulses around me, and soon I've exploded into him.

"God, what a superlative plowing. *Damn*, Daddy, I needed that," Byron gasps as soon as I've gathered sufficient thought to unknot his stick-gag. I fetch a wet washrag to clean us up before uncuffing him. Embracing, we snuggle and drowse in the firelight for a long time. Then Byron sucks me hard again, straddles my waist, sits on my cock with a flinch and a sigh and jacks off on my chest.

Fiction, fiction, sadly fiction. This final sex scene's fact. This last man's real, not fantasized. He's horny, kinky, queer and more than willing. He's versatile, meaning he loves to top cubs but he'll bottom for some guys, including me if I ask nicely. And he's my type, I'm glad to say, a muscle-bear, a Daddybear. True, he'd be hotter if his goatee were less gray, more black; if there weren't those midlife bags under his eyes and lines on his brow; if he could just stop swilling martinis and scarfing doughnuts and lose twenty pounds. But he's burly and butch, a passion-starved mountain man with a solid set of shoulders and arms, a chest molded by decades of weight lifting; he's hairy, though the thick pelt between his pecs is silvery, no longer dark, and his thick arms are covered with intricate tattoos.

Stripped to the waist, head bowed, he stands before the bathroom mirror. Now he lifts his head, looks himself in the eyes and begins. When he ties a camo bandana between his teeth, then plasters a strip of duct tape over his mouth, his cock stiffens inside his boxer briefs. His nipples are prominent after so many blessed years of rough play, and on them he hangs clamps. When he tightens the metal teeth, he simultaneously grunts with pain and grows twice as aroused. Now he drops his briefs and takes his long cock in his hand.

More and more, as a mortal ages, desire is sadly unreciprocated, all about looking, not touching. Eyes must substitute for skin, so to speak, and skin grows more and more irrelevant. But this man, he can see and stroke himself, he likes his own looks, he desires that broad-shouldered Daddy in the glass.

Now he drops his dick long enough to twist both clamps cruelly. Pain knots his brow. He throws back his head and gives a long, muffled moan. Seizing his cock again, he strokes himself harder, palm-skin sliding blissfully over prick-skin, subject for once become object, Top simultaneously bottom, Narcissus bending toward the water to kiss himself. By now, his tits are burning, his cock's a taut sheen, his fist a blur. Lifting one hand, he tugs a tortured nipple, bites down on the bandana knotted between his teeth, locks eyes with the man in the mirror and arches his back. With a hoarse growl, he gushes cum into the sink.

He stands there trembling, panting, relishing the fading frissons of orgasm. Now he gives a baritone chuckle, shakes his head and peels the tape off his stubbly face. Sheepish laughter as he unknots the mouth-moist bandana, a doubled wincing as he eases off the tit clamps. He washes his splattered semen down the drain. Grinning, he studies himself in the mirror, captor admiring captive, Daddy savoring boy. He's still furry, strong, powerful. He's virile yet. He flexes his arms and pecs, runs his fingers through his chest hair and caresses his aching nipples. For a few moments, he has no need of any other.

YOU'VE BEEN SPUNKED

Rob Rosen

I leapt up, plastic cockroaches on either side of me, a stuffed rat with beady pink eyes staring down from my nightstand, my alarm clock blaring at maximum, earsplitting volume. So, fuck yeah, I shrieked like a little girl, wiping the bugs away, rapid-fast, jumping to the side of the bed and away from the rodent, all with a bewildered look of terror etched on my face—all with my roommate's camera pointed my way, the red flashing light indicating that my morning fright-fest was being recorded.

Tom, said roommate, was laughing uncontrollably, filming all the while. "Morning, Steve," he bellowed, tears streaming down his face as I tried to get my breathing back to normal.

"Fuckwad," I yelled, throwing my pillow at him, then the rat, both missing by a mile, my girlie throw also caught on camera, to be shown at some future date to various friends, or worse, on YouTube.

I slammed the clock radio off and hopped up, ready to pulverize him, or at least give chase. But for some bewildering reason, he wasn't running. Instead, he was pointing the camera downward, laughing even louder. "Nice morning woody," he howled. "Thanks for the perfect ending, dude."

I stopped midstep and tried, as best I could, to cover my boxers, my hard-on poking my palm, unwilling to settle down. I mean, come on, Tom was in nothing but a pair of torn sweat shorts, his ripped body glowing in the early morning rays that managed their way through my blinds. Anyway, I jumped back into bed and threw the blanket over my boner. "I'll get you, asshole. Just when you least expect it."

"I'm trembling," he mocked, already turning to leave. "And speaking of assholes, keep that pecker of yours away from mine." Again he laughed, rounding the corner and moving out of sight, his insistent chuckling fading in the distance.

I reached for my still-throbbing prick, my hand inside my boxers giving a yank and a tug while imagining just what he'd said, my cock in his hole, his prick bouncing up and down as he rode me, his head tilted back so I could suck his neck, a tender lobe, all while pulling his heavy nut sac, swirled as it was in all that blond, wiry hair. This distinctive feature of his I knew well enough, seeing as he always wore those same baggy sweat shorts, his balls flopping out, my eyes zooming in when he wasn't paying attention. My mind now had all this streaming in instant replay, my fist pumping away, the come rising up, up, up until it burst out, dousing the inside of my boxers in a heavy load of hot sticky come, my moans muffled by the blanket.

"I'll fucking get you," I repeated, my body twitching, my voice gravelly, my hand working the last few drops of sap from my cock.

I needed a plan. Something devious. Something that would get him back for all the pranks he was constantly pulling on me, make his heart stop for a few seconds. The ultimate punk. And as I was cleaning up my sticky mess, that punk formed in my twisted, revenge-soaked mind. All that was needed was a bit of shopping and good timing.

Luckily, there was a toy store not far from our apartment. Luckier still, Tom went out drinking that night, leaving me to my own devices, with plenty of time to set everything up, make sure the camera was hidden and on and me hidden as well, inside his closet, dressed like a burglar, the toy gun nestled in my front pocket, bandana tied around my neck. I was ready for payback, vengeance soon to be mine.

It was late when he got home. I watched through the closet slats as he flicked the lights on and shut the door behind him. I stifled a laugh as I pictured his shocked reaction, though when he reached into his dresser drawer and pulled out a bottle of lube, I knew I wasn't going to be jumping out of the closet any time soon. I was trapped, but at least I had a promising show ahead of me. My breath caught in my throat, heart pumping madly in my chest, while he unbuttoned his shirt, tossing it to the ground as he kicked off his shoes and rolled off his socks. He was about two feet away from me now, admiring himself in his full-length mirror, flexing his brawny chest, tightening his six-pack, all while I stared, rubbing my cock through my jeans.

He unbuttoned his khakis, sliding them off, his waist eye-level, his briefs noticeably tenting. I'd seen Tom naked before, but never hard, and never from a couple of feet away. I huddled there, mesmerized, my zipper now down, my hand inside, watching as he peeled off his underwear, his cock bouncing, jutting out a good seven inches, the wide mushroom head already slick with precome, his big balls swaying like a pendulum. I reached for something to stifle a groan and was fortunate to find a pair of his underwear, used, musky, smelling of his ass and cock. I pressed them over my mouth while inhaling their stink, my eyelids fluttering, and yanked out my prick while he ogled his perfect body in the mirror. *Vanity, thy name is Tom.* Still, who was I to complain? Lucky me; I had a ringside seat.

He lowered his body to the floor, sidling up to the mirror, out of my line of vision. Slowly, quietly, I stood up, peeked down. His head was propped up by his arm while he watched himself jacking off, his cock slick with lube, gleaming, his heavy balls rising and falling as he beat his meat, the sound of his breathing spiraling around the room, causing my head to spin. I sighed, dropping my jeans and briefs to the ground, matching him stroke for eager stroke.

Another surprise. He raised his magnificent legs and spread them, his asshole winking back at him from the mirror. I pressed my face flush to the closet door, staring hungrily as he rubbed some of the lube around his hair-rimmed hole, his finger sliding in, a moan escaping from his lips, the finger joined by its neighbor, both of them disappearing up his ass. The moan grew louder before being eclipsed suddenly, sadly, by the sound of the closet door swinging open and me tumbling out, cock still in hand, jeans around my ankles, his dirty underwear crammed against my face.

"What the fuck!" he shouted, his hand popping free from his ass as he scooted away, fear and confusion stretched across his face. "Steve!" he hollered a second later.

I reached down to my jeans and removed the toy gun. "Bang," I squeaked.

He jumped up and pounced, not punching me so much as tossing me around, anger evident on his face. And then something else. His hard cock was now butting up against my own, his hands suddenly on my ass, his face an inch from mine, both of us breathing hard. "What the fuck were you doing?" he asked, his voice almost a whisper.

"I wanted to scare you," I mumbled. "To get even."

His scowl turned to a smirk. "This is what you call getting even?"

His lips unexpectedly brushed mine, sending a volt of adrenaline through my body and into my cock, which bounced. "Um, more like unforeseen circumstances," I replied, kissing him in return, softly, my eyes open, watching, waiting, my every nerve vibrating.

He laughed and grabbed my prick. "Dude, this so falls out of the realm of unforeseen." Again he kissed me, hard, insistent, his tongue snaking its way inside my mouth, coiling around my own for a swap of some heavy spit.

I broke an inch away. "Yeah," I chuckled, my hand roaming up and down his back, my fingers running through the soft down just above his ass. "Especially the part where you were finger-fucking yourself."

A splash of crimson brushed his cheeks. "Oh, you, um, saw that, huh?" He began a slow even stroke on my cock.

"Saw it and taped it, if I'm not mistaken."

He retracted his face from mine, but just by a hair. "This is all on film?"

"Digital camera, so, technically, not film. Still..."

Again he laughed. "My first porno role and I've got top billing."

I echoed his laugh with one of my own. "Well, the top part remains to be seen. I mean, it seems to me like you enjoyed those fingers up your ass, dude."

He paused, moving in again, his forehead tilted against mine. "Fingers are one thing, dude. I, um, never had a dick up there before."

I smiled, kissing his nose. "Yet."

He laughed. "Yet. Right."

"Plus, it'll be on film. For posterity's sake."

He rubbed his ass and rolled over on his back. "More like posterior, but you sold me. Fuck away, roomie."

I moved over, leaning against his side, my fingers exploring his peaks and valleys, those areas of his body I'd only ever caught glimpses of before, now suddenly opened up to me for close inspection. "Really? I can fuck you, dude?" The very sound of it sent my blood racing.

He grinned. "Can we hook the computer up to the video recorder, to, um, you know, watch it?"

I chuckled, my cock thickening even more. "You want to watch me fuck you?"

He reached up, his hand stroking my chin before sliding down to pinch a nipple, his thumb and index fingers tweaking and pulling on my sensitive appendage. "Sounds hot, dude. Why not?"

Who could argue with logic like that? I jumped up and retrieved the hidden camera, then ran to my side of the room to get the connecting plug. Minutes later, we were recording, a straight shot right on up to his beautiful hole, the scene unfolding live on his laptop, now positioned to our side.

I zoomed in, his hole filling the screen, pink and perfect, fine blond hairs making a halo around the ring. "Nice," I groaned, staring from the laptop and then back to the real deal.

He raised his legs and spread them again, gazing at his ass as if it were a work of art. All things considered, he wasn't too far off the mark. His fingers quickly began to run circles around the ring, dipping inside just a millimeter at a time. "Cool view." He looked up at me, my face and the lens pressed tight to his ass. "Have a taste, dude."

My head moved in closer, the smell of him wafting up my nose as my tongue darted out, his hole soft like velvet, tasting of sweat, salty sweet. He bucked his ass into my face while I sucked and slurped away, his great big balls bouncing on my forehead while he stroked his thick prick. I glanced above his horizon, his eyes focused on the action on the screen, his mouth open in a pant. I shoved my tongue inside, causing a moan to escape from between his parted lips.

"Fuck, dude," he sighed.

"I was getting to that," I said, the words muffled by his ass.

My mouth moved upward, licking and lapping at the tender spot beneath his sac before sucking on one ball, then the other, my tongue swirling around the glorious expanse of soft, wrinkled skin and fine blond hairs. He thumped his prick against my nose, the one slitted eye staring into my two.

"Suck my cock, dude," he rasped, the last word drawn out in a long, deep exhale.

My head exploded at the sound of it, Fourth of July fireworks flashing behind my eyes, my mouth around his dick a split second later, my lips working their way around the fat head and then down, down, down his pulsing shaft as a happy gagging tear cascaded across my cheek.

"Mm," I practically purred, sucking away.

"Mm," he echoed, pumping his prick down my throat.

I turned my head sideways and watched my progress on the laptop, his meat disappearing and then reappearing, slick with my spit, his balls rising and falling with each slurp, the image giving me a new idea, hotter than the others by far.

I popped his prick out of my eager mouth. "Ready to get fucked, dude?"

He nodded. "Oh, yeah, dude. Hurry up and fuck me already."

I laughed and jumped up, helping him to his feet. "Then you better get me a rubber."

His smile grew bright as he reached into his dresser drawer and pulled out a packet, quickly handing it to me. "Now what?"

I sat down a few feet in front of the mirror, my legs stretched out and apart, and slid the rubber over my erect rod, the lens zoomed in on my crotch, the laptop's screen reflected in the mirror. "Now squat, dude."

He stood in front of me, beautiful ass to smiling face, and did as I asked, bending at the knees, his hand reaching down, the lube already slathered in his palm so that he could slick me up before he lined his portal up with my poker. I held on to his hips and glided him in, just the tip making its way inside, his breath sucking in before he relaxed and allowed the intrusion, sighing long and low and deep as inch after inch of me worked its way to his farthest reaches.

"Okay?" I asked, a million tingles riding up and down my back like a runaway locomotive.

He moaned. "Feels good, dude. Just go slow."

I grinned, my face to the side, staring into the mirror, the image exactly like in my dreams, his head tilted back while he rode my cock, his giant balls bouncing as he stroked his tool, the whole thing blown up on the reflected laptop screen, a close-up of my dick pounding away at his hole, almost too hot to watch. Almost, of course, but not quite.

I looked up from the scene, my eyes locking with his in the mirror. He nodded and smiled, a big toothy grin, then he rose up and slammed his ass down, up and down, again and again and again, each time smashing into my balls, the effect blinding, pleasure mixed with pain, a euphoric combination that sent my cock pumping and grinding even harder into his hole. A sight to see, and, man, was I seeing it from all angles now.

He leaned his head back. I reached my hands around his

waist, my thumbs strumming his solid abs, my face craned up to suck on his neck, a proffered earlobe. "Make me come, dude," he soon rasped.

"No prob, dude," I whispered back.

And then I let him have it with both guns, my cock plunging in, ramming against his granite-solid prostate, both of us panting now, sweat soaked, his hand working feverishly on his dick. "Fuck," he moaned, the sound wrapping around my head as we shot in unison, both of us now staring at the screen, watching his cock explode, the come spewing forth, thick wads of it firing up and out, landing on the carpet, my foot, his thigh, his moans and groans mixing with mine in an ecstatic symphony.

"Fuck," I echoed, my cock rocketing up his ass, filling the rubber up with ounce after creamy hot ounce of jizz, my arms locked around him, holding on for dear life, trying to catch my breath as he did the same, the word *fuck* repeated over and over again.

Eventually, he levered himself up, my dick popping out of his ass, the last drops of come dripping onto my crotch. He helped me to my feet, staring at me sheepishly, and followed with a tender kiss, a stroke of his palm against my cheek. "That was hot, dude," he managed.

"Understatement," I corrected.

Then we hopped into his bed and drifted off to sleep together, his arms wrapped around me in a snug embrace, the scene playing out once again in my dreams, waking me up long after the sun made its daily appearance. I was alone by then, his side of the bed now empty, a note atop his pillow. *Went to get some breakfast, be back in a bit.*

I smiled, absentmindedly stroking my morning woody, and spotted the camera and laptop still sitting on the floor, just as we'd left it. I hopped up, my cock swaying as I bounded over. I hit rewind, then play, the scene no longer in my head; it was on the screen. My dick pulsed at the sight, the moment of entry, his perfect ass impaled. I beat off as I watched, turning up the volume to listen to the sounds of our fucking.

Not loud enough, however, to drown out the noise of his crashing through the closet, nor of me squealing, as usual, like a little girl, jumping away as he bounded out, toy gun pointed my way, the bandana over his mouth, stark naked, hard as a friggin' rock.

"Bang!" he shouted.

I let go of my cock and clutched at my chest. "Fucker!"

He stared from me to the screen. "Next time, dude, I will be."

I grinned, my heart suddenly pumping even harder. "No time like the present." I got on all fours, legs wide, my asshole winking up at him.

I felt his deft tongue glide down my crack. "Present and future, dude." His tongue pushed in and up and back, replaced by a spit-slick index finger, then its neighbor. "And all captured on camera."

I chuckled, stroking my cock, the come already rising from my balls. "Gotta love that posterity's sake thing, dude." His sheathed prick was inside of me in no time flat, filling up every inch of me, until I didn't know where he ended and I began. "Gotta fucking love it."

GOLDEN SHADOWS

David Holly

Bicycling along the island road while wearing only my tropical-print thong swimsuit, I did not encounter any harassment. I waved cheerily at the few passing cars. Most of the drivers waved back, some answering with friendly toots. After seeing my browning skin cycling along that same road every day for the past month, the locals had gotten used to me.

For the first week as I bicycled along the windbreaks of slash pine, royal palm, and sea grape, I was met with jeers and catcalls. Drivers would shout, "Put some clothes on, you freak," or other endearments like "perverted show-off," but the taunts had decreased as familiarity grew. As I pedaled along a narrow shoulder overhung with jacaranda blossoms, the farmer Joe Peters slowed beside me. His two children, Crissy and Bart, greeted me in between giggling at my bare butt.

"Hey, Shannon, our hens laid more eggs than we can eat this week," Joe called. "Stop by later and Margie will give you a dozen."

Thanking the farmer, I pedaled onward. The essence of new-mown hay mingled with the scents of fresh manure, coffee, allspice and papaya, but another smell overwhelmed the others. It was the scent of the sea, and thus I came through a woods of breadfruit and date palms, past brilliant oleanders, crotons, trumpet vines, and hibiscus to the wide sand beach. Even my knobby tires bogged down quickly. I dismounted and walked my bicycle down the golden sands. The waves were placid rollers, and the coconut palms swayed soothingly in the breeze.

Perhaps fifty people occupied the beach, fifty people of all races, all persuasions, all genders. Taking my gay pride beach towel, sunscreen, hat, and bottle of lemonade from my panniers, I looked for the most conspicuous spot. As I scanned the beach, I could not see any serious competition. Being tourists from the United States or Canada, most of the males were wearing knee-length swim shorts that looked like they had been purchased in bulk from a canvas factory. One German was wearing a tight, square-cut boxer and two Russian tourist men were wearing colorful swim briefs. I was the only male decked out in a thong. *Another triumph. Now all the beachgoers must ogle my shape while they anguish over their own sad physiques.*

Of course, I was the only *guy* wearing a thong—not the only human in a thong. Females were present, and the braver wore revealing swimwear. I could do nothing about them, and though some filled, or spilled out of, their swimsuits with slutty neglect, my ass was the most eye-catching lure on the beach. The way my cock and balls filled the pouch of my thong, and the way my gym-hardened butt protruded beyond the cloth that ran deep into my anal cleft were attributes no mere female could match. I had worked for years at the gym, squatting and thrusting upward with ever increasing weights, to turn my natural boy ass into alluring buns of stainless steel.

Yet, not once—not once—in the past month had I met any guy who fully appreciated my body. I had displayed my attributes, but not a single decent-looking man with more than two functioning brain cells had approached me. I stood on the beach as a stranger. Friend to island farmers—yes. Friend to horny gay men who would worship my cock and ass—dream on. The only way any man would touch me, apparently, was if I drowned myself in the blood-warm surf, and they examined my sullied flesh after I was dead.

Entire families and political parties were having better sexual adventures than I was having on that Eden-spun island. Standing on my towel, I completed an impressive series of calisthenics, followed by a routine of gymnastics. Without a doubt, jumping jacks and cartwheels drew eyes to me, but not a single man that I would have.

Sweating with exertion, I sprawled facedown upon my beach towel for an hour. Then I rolled over and toasted the front. I had taken a lot of sun during the past month, and my skin was looking like toast. But it was golden toast, not burnt toast. I kept my body sunscreened against the blistering and peeling, and thus I hoped to let the rays of old Sol tan but not burn. There was the risk of skin cancer, but I was still relatively young and gorgeous. As Horace was fond of saying, "*carpe diem, quam minimum credula postero*," or as John Dryden wrote, "tomorrow do thy worst, for I have lived today."

With that dismissal of the future, I arose to make my customary strut down the beach. The sun was hot on my skin, and the sand was even hotter under my calloused feet, but hottest of all were the eyes upon me. A group of fifty-year-old American women called out lewd comments to me as I strutted, casting a golden shadow in my wake.

"Nice buns."

"Check out his banana hammock."

"Hey, sweetie, come over here."

"He's completely gay, girls. He's not interested in your old asses." That last comment brought an answering smile to my lips. I waved cheerily to the four dames, wiggling my bare buttocks for their benefit.

Pressing on past these admirers, I passed an elderly gentleman who gave me a come-hither look. Had he not been so obese, his white hairs would not have bothered me. I tossed him a grin and a good view of my browning butt as I walked toward the warm waves.

For whatever reason, I noticed the sailor in the sharpie with two dark-red sails. Several sailboats dotted the bay, but this one stood out because I could feel the sailor's hot eyes surveying my body. He tacked toward shore, pulling up his daggerboard as he reached the shallows. The shadow of a gray ray slid under his boat as he drew closer to me, but he appeared not to notice. His eyes were fixed upon the protrusive curvature of my ass.

As the sailboat neared the sandbar, the sailor jumped up to lower the sail. At the sight, my heart leaped into my throat, and my thong tightened in my buttcrack. The sailor was wearing a white sailor's hat, an open blue vest that displayed his tanned and muscled chest, and the tightest white pants I had ever seen on any man. They looked more like paint than fabric.

Of course, women were staring at the sailor, and not a few other men, but his eyes were hot on me. I turned so he had a side view of my bubble butt and my gym-hardened physique. He knew that I was showing off, presenting my assets to all of the beachgoers but particularly to him.

After he threw out his anchor, he bent and rolled the bottoms of his pants. Though his white sailor pants fit his ass and thighs like a second skin, they ended in the traditional sailor's bell-bottoms. I swear that his eyes never left me—he feasted upon my ass as I stood in profile, watching him peripherally. Slipping over the side of his sailboat, he waded to shore. I turned back to him, giving him a good look at my chest and arms. His eyes flickered over my chest, rose to my eyes and drank in my features. I turned on my high-wattage smile. His answering grin was accompanied with a slow eyeballing as he traveled down my body to take in the bulge in my thong. I turned again to give him a bit of profile, and his eyes traveled along my hip with laser-like intent. His eyes smoldered as he stared with palpable lust at my butt curves.

There was nothing of shyness in him. His bare feet left perfect prints in the wet sand as he approached. He was a little swishier in his walk than I first imagined, but I assumed that the tightness of his pants forced out that wiggle. Besides, I am both a looking glass and a window, and the two-sided spirit calls out to the same.

Nevertheless, I have always indulged in a secret fantasy. I've wondered what it would be like to seduce a totally straight man—to attract some guy who believed that he was straight arrow heterosexual all the way—and make him my bitch! I'd like to attract all of the self-doubters and self-loathers, those praying to be straight, those denying their secret lusts, those willing to persecute others for displaying those desires that the persecuted hide within their soul. I would like to attract all of those with my gorgeous gay body, make them service me, and turn them and twist them until they hardly know Shakespeare from a theater seat.

The sailor was not one of those. He radiated gayness in the way a white diamond casts forth the light. "You look great in that thong," he said. "Not every male can wear one, but you carry it off wonderfully."

A heat rushed through me as he admired my body. Great genetics combined with years of training every muscle into the most pleasing curves were paying off for me.

"Do you like looking at me?" I asked coyly.

"I'd like touching you better," he said.

"You would like to stroke me all over?" We were still standing two feet apart, but the sexual tension between us felt like a wave of heat lightning.

"Stroke you. Kiss you. Lick you." The bulge in the crotch of his sailor pants was moving under the white fabric. His tight pants left his cock nowhere to go, but it was trying desperately to rise.

Rising for me, I thought. Rising because my body drew him. Rising from what he perceived only with his eyes, the feast of the sunlit image of my toasted body beaming into his pupils and transmitted as neural impulses back to his brain. I, the feast, stood sprung-hipped in my thong that was pulling tighter into my anal crevice as my cock tightened the stuffed front pouch.

The sailor's hands were moving toward me, appearing to slip in slow motion through the hot scented air. "Did Mae make it for you?" he murmured. He was talking about my thong again. "Those brilliant tropical colors. That bougainvillea design in the fabric. Not something any straight man would ever wear."

That was the truth. I had gone to Mae's shop and asked for the gayest-looking thong she carried. Mae cut and sewed the fabric on the spot, fitting it to my naked body.

"Make it reflect the flamboyant gaiety of my spirit."

"Are you a top or a bottom?" Mae asked nosily as she threaded the fabric between my bare buttocks.

"I'll bet you ask that of all the boys."

"I do. So which are you? Do you pitch or catch? Do you ride or drive?"

"Both—and neither," I said. "I like to show off my body. I am an actor."

The sailor's fingers were still moving toward my taut pouch when a sudden commotion arrested the moment. Caught in that magical moment, neither the sailor nor I had detected the whine of the vintage 1930s DC3 float plane. We did notice the shower of paper raining down upon us, the millions of pieces of greenish rectangular paper that filled the air and covered the beach. And, of course, we noticed the terrific explosion at the far end of the island as the plane crashed into the dunes, scattering debris and sending a fireball skyward.

The beachgoers were numbed at first, awestruck at the obviously fatal catastrophe and staggered by the rain of hundred-dollar bills that covered the beach like so much trash. The sailor and I stood in the midst of the breeze-borne cash dropped from the so-recently-dead drug dealers' crashing aircraft. Neither of us commented on the money. We hardly glanced at it, except to note that the litter was besmirching the natural beauty. However, the beachgoers were eager to clean up the trash. Within a few minutes an insane free-for-all developed. Half-clothed people were madly dashing to and fro, gathering up more cash than they could hold in their hands. Some were wrapping money up in blankets and beach towels, while others stripped naked to convert their swimsuits into purses.

A naked woman slammed into me in her deranged dash to clutch the bills swirling around my feet. I fell forward and the sailor caught me.

"Perhaps we'll be safer on my boat," he suggested.

Would anyone see me there? For a flash of a moment, I almost refused. However, no one was seeing me then anyway, so rapt were the beachgoers in scooping up the cash. I let the sailor take my hand and pull me toward the warm salt.

"The warm salt," I murmured to myself, enjoying his attention while lamenting that I was no longer the cynosure of all eyes on the beach.

"Warm salt is a strange metonymy," the sailor said as we waded in to our knees.

"Are you an English professor?"

"How did you guess?"

"You're too literate to be anything else." I told him my name and where I taught. His name, I learned, was Craig Warren, a professor of classical studies at Elmwood College.

"Shannon Wright," I said as we climbed into his sharpie sailboat. "I specialize in sixteenth-century drama, and I am head of the theater department at Multnomah State University."

Craig looked me up and down with some amazement. I had advanced to my position young, and though a few years had passed, I still looked younger than my actual years. Self-discipline at table and bar had helped, as had countless hours building muscle, increasing endurance, and improving agility and balance. I could still perform a prattfall that would have an audience rolling in the aisles.

"I had you tagged as being totally into yourself," Craig observed, mimicking his students' speech.

"Oh, I am. I like to show myself. I am a college professor, a theater director and an actor. I show off my body, my sexuality, my talent. Hence the thong." I stuck out my ass in demonstration. "Else why the stance? Who wouldn't expect an actor to have a narcissistic personality?" I grinned to show that I possessed the humility to appreciate and mock my egoistic desire for attention. "I still teach classes, and I put on quite a show for my students. I enjoy the attention, but I teach a coherent, instructive and meaningful lesson every time."

"Do your students know that you're gay?"

I could not help but laugh. "From what you have seen of my behavior so far, do you imagine that any of my students are left in doubt? I'm an actor. A director. A drama coach. I sing, I dance, I perform gymnastics and I am equally comfortable in Oscar Wilde's suit with the green carnation, or Robin Hood's tights, or James Dean's jeans, or Randolph Scott's shirt."

"And whose thong is that?" Craig asked, his hands sliding down my back until his probing fingers slid over the rising mounds of my ass and his hot palms cupped my buttocks.

"It's a Shannon Wright thong." His touch sent thrills through me. My asshole tightened, as did my cock. I shuddered. Turning slightly I saw my fellow beachgoers still scrambling for dough. Nevertheless, even if they did not see, if they did not observe, if they did not care, I resolved to put on the best possible show. They would see this sailor pleasure me. They would see—if not with their faces' eyes, then with their minds' eyes—they would see him worship my ass, worship my muscles, worship my cock. They would see it all enacted in this sharpie sailboat, even though their eyes were fixed upon the false promise of cash from an exploded drug plane.

A younger guy who had pulled off his flowery board shorts bumped against the side of our vessel. He was most desperately plucking bills from the water around us and making his former swimsuit into a money bag. Laughing at the naked greed, Craig slid his hands over my ass again.

"Worship my cock," I suggested.

He stiffened. He wanted to worship my ass instead, but he would settle for my cock. "Do you want to pour your cum into me?"

"Oh, yes. Make me part of you. Suck my cock. Suck me until I come. Swallow my essence."

Without further ado, Craig pulled my thong down to my

knees. I stood so he could remove it from me entirely, and so all the beach would see my naked skin. Too absorbed in gathering the money from the flaming drug plane, each man, woman and child scrambled naked, clothed or otherwise for the cocaine-crusted bills. Craig kissed my cock's head with his seaworthy mouth, and I closed my eyes as a tremendous weakness claimed me. "Oh, Craig," I mouthed, hardly able to speak.

"Let me do everything, Shannon," Craig said withdrawing his mouth briefly from my cock. "Don't try to help. Give your cock to me."

As if I would deny my cock and cum to him! Whatever Craig was willing to do, so was I eager to give or to receive.

"My cock is yours," I whispered as his hands slipped over the mounds of my naked ass. "And let all the world watch in awe."

Craig kissed and licked my shaft before going to work in earnest on my dickhead. He massaged the tip of my cock with hot firm lips. His mouth worked me, encased me, enraptured me. In rapture, my spirit drifted over the sapphire shallows toward the unfathomable indigo deeps. When his tongue caressed my cock, I thought I'd expire from the breathtaking distress of yet unfilled pleasure. I hovered on the rim of insensible delight, unable to move and hardly able to breathe. My cock was hard near to splitting; I leaked lean streams into Craig's mouth.

"Worship my cock," I gasped. "Give me your adoration."

Like an angel at the gates of paradise, Craig took my whole cock then. His mouth was a tight, moist thing that encased my cock. His mouth was a sucking pleasure hole. "Uh," I moaned, unable to form coherent thoughts or words. His mouth sucked me toward the by then crucial orgasm. "Ah," I gasped, hardly drawing breath as billows of staggering pleasure swept through my loins. All my narcissistic, attention-seeking soul condensed in my balls. My mouth murmured words of its own accord. "Feel me. Taste me."

I tried to stand so the beachgoers could see my naked butt-crack, but Craig pushed me down. His lips pressed against my shaved pubic area. I wanted to stand. I wanted to be watched, but I allowed myself to be driven farther down toward the floor of the sailboat.

Standing firm would have been nothing more than a toothless chomp at a steak sandwich. The lust for money is the root of all human vacuity. I could have been waving roman candles while Craig blew me and no one would have noticed then.

"Oh, Craig," I whimpered as the orgasmic waves deepened, and I was caught in a tornado of pleasure. The potent muscles at the base of my penis contracted as they'd never constricted during masturbation before the mirror, and I savored the great spurt of cum springing forth from my cock and chugging down Craig's throat. I no longer cared whether anyone watched me or admired me. My very narcissism, the seat of my personality, pumped from my balls, flooded up my dick stem, and poured into the sucking mouth of a sailboating English professor. The waves of rapture rolled on and each came with that intensely satisfying ejaculation of my life's spunk.

In some mysterious way, strange and delicious, the realization that I was coming into Craig's mouth made me wonder whether I might grow from object to admirer. Would I soon be the one giving the blow job to him? Would I be receiving his cock in my mouth or even in my ass? Would I be able, for once in my life, to think of giving pleasure to another?

Black smoke was still pouring from the scene of the plane crash, but we were spared the odors. Obviously the drug smugglers had perished in the crash, but no one on the beach attempted to check. They were too busy searching for any remaining hundred-dollar bills. Neither Craig nor I had devoted an iota of thought to the victims either. We had been too absorbed in our own bliss.

Bicycling back to my rented bungalow, I stopped at Joe Peters's farm for the eggs. Margie eyed my thong with amusement as she helped me store the eggs in my bicycle's pannier. The kids, Crissy and Bart, did not giggle then. Joe came out of the barn, and Margie pointed toward my swimsuit. "You ought to buy one like it, Joe. You could wear it around the farm. Set a new trend among the island farmers."

"I bought it at Mae's shop in the village," I offered helpfully. "She'll make you one. It'll be the perfect fit." Margie laughed at that, but Joe turned bright red. The kids looked at their father anxiously as if they expected him to put on a thong right then.

Taking leave of the family, I bicycled up the hill at the island's center. The air temperature dropped about ten degrees as I climbed, but the cooler air felt pleasant upon my skin. I reached my bougainvillea-covered bungalow, put my bicycle in the storage shed, and carried my fresh eggs inside.

The island taxi service car arrived right at seven, and Craig climbed out. He had changed out of his sailor suit and was wearing sneakers, tight denim shorts, and a muscle shirt. I kissed him warmly, somewhat to the taxi driver's surprise, and ushered him inside.

"I see you took off your thong," Craig said, surveying my naked cock. Perhaps it was the full frontal view that had caused the taxi driver's eyes to bulge so oddly.

"I hardly ever wear clothes around the house."

Laughing, Craig pulled off his sneakers, pulled his shirt over his head and skimmed off his shorts. To my delight, he wasn't wearing underwear. I pressed close and kissed him again. He placed his hand behind my head and held me in the kiss until both of our cocks were rigid. His other hand slid down my back until he caressed my ass.

"I do worship your ass, Shannon."

"I know. But we'll eat dinner first. I have everything ready."

I poured glasses of a frosty chardonnay flavored with a hint of coconut, and led him to a table already prepared in my backyard. The sun was just setting over the golden shadows of the sea. I lit a couple of citronella candles to keep the night's insects away.

Craig looked about nervously. "Are you sure that your neighbors can't see us? We're pretty exposed to be naked."

"Oh, they can see us just fine. Don't worry about it. Since I started the trend earlier this summer, most of them have been going about in the buff too."

"Who needs clothes in this climate?" Craig asked rhetorically and a little falsely. He was not used to public nudity.

We sipped our wine and forked chunks of the crayfish salad into our mouths. I rescued a gigantic round of flat bread from the oven, which we dipped in olive oil. Red snapper broiled with dill followed, and dessert was a tart lime cheesecake. We sampled everything but we did not drink to excess, nor did we surfeit ourselves with the food. The night promised other pleasures.

Craig and I came together under the rising moon. I kissed his lips and let his tongue probe my mouth. Our lips pressed, warred, struggled, caressed, made love. He licked the inside of my lips. I stabbed my tongue into his mouth, fucking it with my tongue as I had fucked it with my cock earlier. Then I sucked his tongue before licking his throat. Olive oil had dripped onto his chest, so I licked it off.

"Do I need to give you a good licking?" he asked me.

I was burning for him. "If you want to. If it pleases you to do so. But that is not the end of this night."

"Oh, I hope not. What do you have in mind, Shannon?"

"I'm going to give you what you want most." What I wanted most too. I wanted him to master me, overpower me, use me. I was ready to give my deepest mysteries to him.

His breath came in a sharp gasp. "You mean..."

"Yes, I'm going to give you my ass. Just the way you want it. With protection or without as you decide."

His eyes widened. "You trust me that much?"

"Speak truth to me, and I will believe you."

"I'm clean. I have no diseases. I've lived a life of extreme caution."

"So have I, Craig."

He regarded me with eyes that spoke so much. "Then you really want to take it bareback this time?"

"Believing in you with all my heart—yea."

"The everlasting yea," he quoted as I led him to my bedroom and he saw the gigantic bed hanging from six thick chains from the bolts in the eight-inch-thick roof beams. I had already arranged two pillows to raise my backside for his enjoyment, and the towels and lubricant lay upon the hibiscus-flowered sheets.

I tumbled into the bed ahead of him and offered him a view of the object of his desire. The bed swung from side to side as he climbed in and placed his hands upon his prize.

"Worship my ass, Craig," I urged, and he gave it his full attention with such devotion that he fed my ego until far into the night.

Craig started by kissing my buttcheeks. Then he kissed my anal crevice and pushed his face between my buttocks, driving his nose and lips into my crack. He slurped up my fissure until his tongue bathed the small of my back. Then he licked downward until he reached my ball sac. As he tongued my buttcrack, his pure need burned within him.

His tongue touched my anal sphincter, the *sigil* of adoration.

I sighed with joyous gratification. As Craig rimmed around my hole, my cock nearly exploded. His adulation delivered me into a state of rapture. Craig idolized me. He adored me, he worshipped my ass.

Craig ravished my anal cleft until my cock throbbed with rhapsody. He licked me and he finger-fucked my ass. However, when he tried to push two fingers into my asshole, I dissuaded him: "Be careful, Craig. You're going to make me come too soon. I love the way you finger-fuck my butt, but I want your cock now. Stick it in, please."

Craig shifted his position. I could feel his burning lust, and then I felt his cock between my rounded buttcheeks. Bareback! I had never taken a cock bareback. I could only wonder at what I was doing.

Closing my eyes and drawing a deep breath, I pushed my asshole open. Craig's cock filled my dilating ass. My own cock throbbed. He started humping me, fucking my ass with a steady rhythm. As he fucked me, his cock milked my prostate, and that combined with my extreme arousal brought me closer to orgasm.

I ground Craig's cock with my asshole, which made him quicken his thrusts. Stirred by the rising semen in his balls, he rode my ass harder and faster. His cock swelled thicker as I tormented it with my asshole. I felt the first tingles that signaled the approaching storm of pleasure.

"You're making me come, Craig," I moaned, as our bed swung upon its chains.

Gripping hard with my buttocks and asshole, I let his cock bring me off. The tingles in my dick surged into bliss. Then I was coming; my hard cock spurting onto my hibiscus-flowered sheets and pillow. In the throes himself, Craig humped me like a maniac, his breath rasping in my ear.

"Come in me," I urged. "Give it to me, Craig. Shoot it into my ass."

I sensed his hot spunk being spurted into me. I felt his cock in my asshole, his hips striking my buttocks, and the continuing deep prostate massage. Following his unbelievably extended orgasm, Craig slowed his thrusts. He pushed his cock in and out a few more times, slowly, ever slowing; then he stopped and lay still. For a minute he stayed atop me with his cock buried in my ass, both of us gasping and sweating. Then we rolled apart and stared at each other with amazement.

"Let's shower together," I suggested, leading him to the shower stall tiled with seashells. "We'll soap each other up and towel each other off."

For years now, Craig and I have corresponded several times a day and telephoned each other frequently. We meet on the island every summer for a full three or four months, but we keep our college professions in different parts of the country. Each summer as we share bungalow, swinging bed, sharpie sailboat, and island bicycling, we also share our cum, giving and receiving, each man in his own way, as the golden shadows of the tropical paradise lengthen across the sapphire sea.

THE PICKUP MAN

Shane Allison

I'm relieved I'm able to make it to Billy's in my piece-of-shit car. It crackles over rock and gravel as I make my way into the parking lot. A week ago it wouldn't start when I was leaving the baths. The last thing I wanted was to call my dad to tell him the carburetor was acting up again and he'd have to pick me up from a bathhouse. He's already embarrassed that I can't tell a flat tire from a dead battery. What can I say? All I know how to do is put gas in 'em and drive 'em.

When I open the thick wooden door, Lynard Skynard blasts out of the hole-in-the-wall country-western bar that's on the ass end of Tallahassee. It's a popular spot for local rednecks, not to mention a slew of cops who get called at least twice a week to break up a fight between a couple of drunken hicks. When I enter, I get more than a few stares, all eyes dead set on burning a hole the size of Florida clean through me.

The place reeks of stale beer and prejudice. I carefully tear past grungy denim-clad cowboys with bloodshot eyes to make my way to the bar. I sandwich myself tightly between two drunkards nursing a couple of longnecks. They look me over disgustedly, as if I don't belong there. And to be honest, Billy's is the last joint I want my black ass to be caught dead in. I stick out like a sore thumb in my Timberlands and baggy FUBUs. I wait and watch the burly bartender pop tops off bottles of cold German beer before I wave him down. He gives me a stern glare. I yell through the brash country tunes roaring from the jukebox that sits against a wall of cinder blocks, "Excuse me. Where's your bathroom?" I hold out my oil-soiled hands. He points past ten-gallon-hooded heads to the far end of the bar. I saunter past mean, prying eyes that continue to watch me as if I'm going to magically sprout wings from my ass.

I press the door open to the men's room where a bunch of cowboys stand side by side at the urinal trough. My dick twitches in my baggy jeans to the sizzle of piss splashing against the glossy porcelain. Some turn to take a look at the new addition; others focus on emptying their bladders. At the sink, I turn the tap with the side of my hand, careful not to smudge it with oil. Cowboy after cowboy enters the shitter, each with a dick full of piss. I'm a bundle of nerves in this den of country boys. I press pink liquid soap into my dirty palms and work it into a frantic lather.

My dick gets thick as I gawk at the row of tight, redneck booties flexing and farting in jeans. I rinse the soap off my hands as I run them under a tongue of cold water. I stare at these muscular, big-butt cowboys as streams of gold shower the trough. I gotta pee so bad I'm about to explode—I've been holding it in since I left home, thinking I could wait until I got to Brian's party. A space opens up between two guys, and I quickly elbow my way between them. "Sorry," I tell them, as I take my place alongside their flannel-clad bear bodies.

As I unzip and fish my dick out of my underwear, I nonchalantly take a peek at soft peckers the size of Vienna sausages being shaken clean of pee. Others are fully erect with cockheads of all shapes and sizes. Some have the typical mushroom head while others are simply cloaked in tender pink foreskin. Some dicks are riddled with veins; others look sweaty and ripe from being held captive in briefs all day. Some even sport Prince Albert crowns. I want nothing more than to drop to my knees and worship each and every erection in all its glory.

I feel a slight burn as I make my own donation into the golden river. I watch for prying eyes to see if any of these country ruffians are checking out my equipment. I'm not what you'd call "porn-star big," but I hold my own, and the boys don't complain. I don't care if they're looking. I'm a dirty little exhibitionist anyway. *Like what you see?* I think. Several of the men have come and gone and have hauled out into a vortex of Brooks and Dunn vibrating against paneled walls and the shoddy Sheetrocked ceiling.

There are only three of us left draining the last droplets from the slits of our dicks. A short, pudgy Mexican dude wearing a cream-colored cowboy hat and caramel-brown boots has finished up, tucking his uncut dick into a tomb of boxers. The medium-build guy to the right of me wears a red and black long-sleeve flannel shirt, a gray cowboy hat, and faded jeans with holes in the knees. He's got a round, bubble, black-boy booty that's firm in dirty denim. His dick is cut, the head slightly freckled. We stand together, close as any two men can get, each playing with ourself for the other to see. I watch excitedly as his dirty fingers squeeze his curved dick.

Just when he's about to grab my cock, two men walk in and take their places next to us. The cowboy nervously puts away his boner and saunters to a vacant sink to wash up. I swaddle my sex back into my Hanes and duck into a stall that's filled with wads of wet toilet paper and soggy cigarette butts. I unroll some tissue and try to clean the toilet rim of pee and what can only be described as tobacco that has been spewed from the dirtiest mouth in town.

A hole's been gutted in the wall of the stall to the left of me. The partition is caked with mostly racist and homophobic graffiti: NIGGERS GO HOME and DIE STALL FAGS. An intricate picture of a Confederate flag has been drawn above the glory hole. The best part of public shitters is reading the ridiculous messages guys scribble while they're pinching a loaf. Some people have way too much time on their hands. I'm one to talk, though, since I'm guilty of sprawling my own dirty messages across bathroom walls.

I push my jeans around my knees to keep them from dragging across the disgusting floor. As I hear the heels of the cowboy's boots against the tile, I stoop over to watch a pair of cruddy snakeskins make their way into the stall next to mine. My glasses graze against the partition. I take them off and stuff them into my shirt pocket. I play with myself as I watch him undress from the waist down. He takes his dick out, then wraps his fingers around it, giving me a state-of-the-art glory-hole show. I glide my index finger within the circle, letting him know I hunger for what hangs between his thick, hairy thighs.

I watch as his crotch comes through the hole. I tilt the soft-hanging member under my nose to give it my infamous smell test. I approve, and work the rest of it past my lips and into my warm mouth. My tongue slithers along the belly of his snake. The traffic from new visitors is thick, but we're both locked securely in our stalls. Some piss and leave, while others linger, as if they know what's up. I struggle to keep my slurping to a minimum by wrapping my lips tighter around his stuff.

Suddenly he uncorks his dick from my mouth. With traces

of drool at the corners of my yapper, I watch for his next move. "Let's go back to my truck," he whispers through the hole, his breath reeking of booze. I make out a coarse brown mustache that covers his top lip. We hurry to make ourselves decent, so much so that my dick nearly catches in the copper jaws of my zipper. When I exit the stall, there's a new row of bodacious cowboys taking leaks, but I couldn't care less.

My dick guides me past a school of pool-playing, beer-guzzling men and into a poorly lit lot of cars, jeeps, and dirty four-by-fours. Whether my crappy car will crank or not is the last thing on my mind. I turn the corner of a green Dumpster to find a pickup near the fence with its parking lights on. It's caked with dried mud. I walk to the front of the truck. THE PICKUP MAN is painted in neat letters across the top of the windshield. I try to make out the cowboy's face through his dark-tinted windows. He pushes open the passenger-side door, but I'm hesitant to get in: I don't know this guy from Adam, and his truck reeks of dead deer.

"How's it goin'?" I ask.

"Hey," he replies. It's dark in the parking lot, but I can make out some of his features.

"That was hot back there," I tell him, even though I'm a bit uneasy about all this. Suddenly I feel like a fly in this dude's web, thinking maybe he's out to spill a punk's blood and leave me for dead in a ditch off some lonely highway. *Don't be stupid,* I think.

"I know a place we can go," he says gruffly.

I usually don't get into cars with guys I don't know—especially guys driving big-ass pickups with tinted windows—but he's a piece of ass too good to pass up. When guys start talking about going back to their place, I usually change my mind and get the hell outta Dodge. Cars with tinted windows really freak me out. A month ago, a local girl was raped and sodomized after she accepted a ride from a stranger. Cops describe the vehicle as a white van with blue stripes and dark windows. They still haven't found the bastard.

"I don't know about going anywhere," I tell him. I look around nervously to study my surroundings just in case this guy tries to kidnap my ass.

"It's cool. I ain't weird or nothin'," he tells me.

After careful consideration, I make up my mind to go along, and I climb into the cab of his pickup. Besides, I have a switchblade in case this motherfucker wants to kick up some shit. I don't want to have to cut a bitch, but I will if things get critical. "Lead the way," I tell him. My heart beats heavy as his truck bucks slowly out of the lot. He drives farther and farther out of the clutches of the city limits, past greasy spoons and signs with store names that end in "4 Less."

"So where we goin'?" I ask him.

"There's a rest stop off Highway 10," he says. "Don't worry. We're almost there."

The pickup roars like a mythical beast as he presses deep into the gas, making his way down a dirt road that slices apart a wooded area off the bustling freeway. There are a few cars in sight, and the ruffian jostles his pickup between two of them, neither of which is occupied by the drivers.

"Dude, is this safe?" I ask.

"It's pretty quiet 'round this time of night. Come on. Let's go in back." He lets down the tail end of the truck exposing the bed strewn with tools and sawed-off pieces of paneling. I press the knife in my pocket, ready to pull it out in case he tries anything. I can't help thinking of the van-driving rapist. "Hop in," he says. "Just push some of this shit off to the side."

As I crawl in on my knees, pushing junk out of the way, he

grabs my ass and presses a finger in the crevice of my butt. He climbs in behind me and collapses into a nest of heavy, hard things that pushes into our flesh. He takes off his cowboy hat and tosses it inside the truck on the seat. Feathers of sweaty black hair are exposed, along with a touch of gray in his brows. His pot roast of a gut is snug under his T-shirt, which displays a pit bull bearing its teeth beneath a Confederate flag. His nipples are pert under the cotton. Like erasers, these things. His big metal belt buckle hangs limply from his waist as he unzips his Wranglers. I watch as he pulls the snakeskin boots off his tube sock–covered feet. "Aintcha gonna get undressed?" he asks.

"I don't know about this, man. Somebody might see us out here."

"It's cool," he assures me. "Nobody'll fuck with us."

He starts to unbutton my shirt with his gritty fingers. It doesn't take me long to get out of my clothes. We're both still in our socks and underwear when he asks me what I'm into.

"Well, you already know I like to suck," I tell him. "I'm pretty versatile, really. I'll try almost anything once."

He reaches into the cotton crotch panel of his briefs and pulls out the dick I'd worshiped a short while ago in the crapper at Billy's. "Anything, huh?" he says. He peels his briefs off hulking legs and tosses them in a nowhere-special direction. A salt-and-pepper thicket surrounds his horse-hung erection. Compared to this rough, redneck of a thing, I have nothing much to offer between my legs.

When I move in to give his nipples a taste test, the congestion in the bed of his truck shuffles beneath my bare, black ass. They blush as I bite and suck them with love. "Ow, fuck!" he yells.

I move between his thighs and take his dick in my nervous palm. His ball sac is tender and coarse. He runs his hands through the kinky crop of my hair as I manhandle his nipples.

"Suck me, boy," he demands, pushing me with force past his beer belly. I waste no time putting his dick in my mouth. I nuzzle my nose in his nest of cowboy-crotch stink. "Awesome, man!" he says. "You suck purty good."

His calling me "boy" gets me hot, causing my dick to thicken even more as I struggle not to gag on his sex. I want him to know I can take a dick proper like a good boy. We turn our bodies in a sixty-nine position. He spreads his legs as I lick along the shaft and suckle the tender goose-bump flesh of his sac. His sweaty hair is cold against the inside of my thigh as he devours my cock. His teeth graze against it, but what's hot sex without a little pain? I brace myself each time his choppers skim along my dick.

"Roll on over, boy. On your back," he says.

My knees point up to the stars as he services me with unrelenting fervor. I squeeze his booty as he runs my dick in and out of his mouth again. He's ripe and sweaty as I glide my tongue along his cherry. "Oh, man, that's awesome. Do that," he says.

He leisurely works his burly butt upon the throne of my face. *There you are, Daddy,* I think, tongue-tickling his button. His dick grazes my chest as I munch away on his butt. The tip of my ring finger slides in easily up his wet stuff. I'm careful not to damage his goods, for his butt is as precious to me as the night sky. I lick and spit continuously on the cowboy's sphincter, fucking him with four fingers, which go up him without a hitch.

"You wanna fuck me, boy?" I'm too busy with his backside to answer. "I wanna fuck."

"You got a rubber?" I ask him.

The cowboy grabs the leg of his jeans and drags them toward our nude bodies. He feels around in one of the pockets and pulls out a cellophane packet. He tears it with his teeth then uses his mouth to roll the prophylactic over my sex. He pulls his cheeks apart with calloused, cruddy fingers, and my dick slides easily up his country ass. In amazement I watch as his walls gorge on my dick.

"Oh, man that's it," he announces. I claw his butt as he rides me like one of those mechanical bulls back at Billy's. Beads of sweat trickle from his furry back as I thrust my sex up his butt with wild abandon. "God, fuck!" he yells.

I never thought I was that great at fucking, but with all the cursing and fussing this hick is doing, I guess I'm not as bad as I thought. I give him a reach around, tugging on his dick like a cow's udder. "Yeah, like that," he says. "I'm close."

The screwing and jerking is in perfect synchronization. "Let's nut together," I tell him.

His moans are sweet music to my ears. "Um comin'," he announces.

You and me both. When I expectedly feel something warm between my fingers, I tug his dick, milking him of every drop. My breaths are heavy; my gluteus maximus muscles ache and burn. I yell silently in my dirty mind that I'm about to come. I brace against his bear shoulders as I climax up his ass, into the flesh-colored rubber. My body relaxes as he slides off my cock.

"You sure can fuck," he says breathlessly.

With aching muscles, we rest for a while before getting dressed. I slap him on the butt as he pushes a foot into one of his boots. When we climb back into the cab, the windshield has fogged with the night's cold. He wipes it clear and drives me back to Billy's, where the graveled lot is empty except for my car parked on the side of the bar.

He pulls in front of Spears Seafood, where they have a sale on roe and oysters, and asks if we could get together again. I scribble my cell number on the back of an old grocery receipt. His 'stache pricks my face when he leans over and kisses me on the cheek.

My car stalls a few times but successfully cranks up after the fourth attempt. “Thank you, baby,” I say, kissing its steering wheel.

I’m not even home yet before my cell phone rings.

“Hello?”

“Hey.” It’s the cowboy. “I forgot to tell ya I had a good time.”

I laugh and assure him that I, too, had fun. We make a date to meet at a bar-and-grill place that’s a tad classier than Billy’s. I get home and collapse on the bed with his cowboy-bear scent on me like cheap cologne.

WHAT PLEASES HIM MOST

Thomas Kearnes

I needed to be numb before surrounding myself with nude, wandering men. The previous times Cutter and I journeyed to the bathhouse in Dallas, I shot through the halls of rented rooms, past the bank of grimy oblong windows overlooking the outdoor pool, through the steam room, beside the hot tub. I cleared them like hurdles. I only went because Cutter so enjoyed all the waiting flesh on display. Yes, occasionally I found a man to bring back to our room that was bought by the hour, but honestly, I would've been just as happy had Cutter been the only man lying beside me, fucking me, loving me. But even with him near me, I needed the tweak to keep me from abandoning my skin, leaving Cutter alone with the strange men while I scurried back home to Denton.

Cutter and I sat on his bed passing the pipe. Posters of great Greek landmarks covered his walls. While a twittering blue jay outside his bedroom window distracted him, I snuck another hit off the pipe.

"Careful with that, boy," he said, gaze not leaving the window. "You don't wanna get so high you can't get hard."

Caught, I simply grinned. Cutter always found me out. Perhaps that was a condition of love. "Why do you think I always bottom?"

"Because that's what I expect from you, boy."

I laughed and passed the pipe. Cutter was always good to me. He volunteered his house in uptown Dallas for our weekends and occasional weeknights together. I still lived in a dorm in Denton, sharing it with a nosy kid from the East Coast. True, Cutter was thirty-seven, but I did my best not to think what would happen, how that age gap would bend and flex into something more obscene if we managed to stay together after these first few months. When he reached fifty, I would be thirty-three. Perhaps an attorney, if I followed my father's urging to attend law school. These frequent trips to the Dallas Spa were the price of admission, I told myself, the price of procuring a boyfriend as accomplished, sexy and—well—manly as Cutter Drake.

My boyfriend was gorgeous, and I wasn't the only one who thought so. During trips to the bathhouse, I watched the way men never stopped walking past but allowed their heads to slowly turn, keeping their eyes on Cutter as he continued the opposite way. He had a fantastic body. He liked to call me from the twenty-four-hour gym downtown and brag whenever he managed to max more weight while pumping iron. But it was his face—the way his smile spread like melting butter: that was where I sometimes caught myself gazing while his attention was elsewhere. The slim, sharp nose; the pale-gray eyes; the long locks of rust-colored hair that flopped down past his eyebrows. And best of all, he was a *man*—masculine and confident, not like those prissy, shaven boys that trolled the sidewalks in Oak Lawn.

"Just a few more hits," I said. "You know, to fortify me."

"You and your big words."

"I'm sorry, but that place...you know..."

He scooped the long end of the pipe into the tiny plastic bag of tweak, ushered another rock into its mouth. "Yes, Darren, I'm aware of your feelings about the bathhouse."

"I'm sorry."

"We don't have to go."

"But you love it there."

"I love watching other men fuck you."

"Do you think we could make it just the two of us today?"

Cutter grinned, cuffed me behind the ear. "All depends on who we find, my boy."

I tried my best to smile. Granted, Cutter never forced any man on me. I got final approval on each trick we invited to our rented room. But always at some point while the chosen man was inside me, Cutter taking snapshots with his digital camera, I began to drift. I thought about how Cutter would fuck me after this strange man left, what he would say to me, how he would praise my "performance." I knew I was doing these things, these men, for *him*—not for myself. But whenever I broke away from the fuck to look at Cutter's face, I saw the pride and lust in his eyes and in that moment believed there could be no higher calling than pleasing the man who loved you.

"It'll be past four when we get there," I said. "We'll be hours ahead of the club crowd."

"Too many fucking twinks at night. The guys that go in the afternoon are *men*."

"Like you," I said.

"Like me." And with that, he pulled me close and kissed me so softly, I felt my heart drop into my stomach. The blue jay twittered again outside the bedroom window. I listened to its panicked cries as Cutter eased me down onto the bed. He set down the pipe on the nightstand and came to rest on top of me. Perhaps we wouldn't make the bathhouse till five that afternoon.

Every weekend we went to the Dallas Spa, Cutter carried an old black gym bag. Inside were all the necessities needed to spend the next few hours fucking strangers: lubricant, condoms, bottles of Gatorade, cock rings, a camera, a tweak pipe and about an ounce of white crystals. We strolled down Swiss Avenue, staring straight ahead. Our first time there, Cutter warned me it was considered impolite to make eye contact with any man leaving the building. Frankly appraising the men should wait until you were in the halls, among the rooms. Or in the steam room or sauna. Anywhere beyond the check-in desk was fair game. At the time, I didn't see the sense behind the rule, but I did as Cutter instructed, not looking up when I felt the gaze of a muscled guy passing us. Today, there was no one leaving when we arrived. Cutter joked with the skinny man behind the check-in counter. He flashed his credit card then collected our room key and the threadbare white terry-cloth towels. We would wear them after shedding our clothes in the rented room. Our check-in complete, Cutter grandly swung out his arm to hold open the swinging door. I chuckled at his mock chivalry and entered the bathhouse.

We first passed through the lounge. It was very large, a pool table at one end and at the other an arrangement of couches and chairs placed before a big-screen television. Cutter once told me the men who gravitated here were either too ugly to fuck or too wired to seek it out. A Cameron Diaz movie played to the small group of bare-chested men seated around the set. My gaze fell on one of the men. He was maybe forty with a solid build.

Coarse chest hair partially obscured his admirable physique. He swiveled his head and caught me staring at him. I quickly averted my gaze, but Cutter had noted our awkward exchange.

"Already on the prowl, boy?"

"No, I just...I thought I knew him."

"Probably saw him here before."

"I'm sure that's it." I forced my voice to brighten, like an airline attendant announcing how to save your own damn life. "Did you get us the VIP room?" I asked.

"You'll just have to follow me and see where I go," Cutter purred and grabbed my wrist, pulling me into the curved hallway connecting the lounge to the small maze of halls and rented rooms. We passed by the stone archway leading to the hot tub, showers and sauna room. I'd go there soon enough. Cutter always insisted I shower after every fuck, no matter how brief. Built into the stone hallway was a series of windows looking out over the kidney-shaped pool and stone sundeck. It was an overcast autumn day, so no men were using the deck chairs. As we neared the maze's entrance, I heard the awful staccato beat of electronic house music thud over the speakers, fill the hallways. I never understood gay men's obsession with remixing perfectly good songs until they all sounded alike. But in my state of intoxication, I found the steady thump of the bass strangely soothing. I imagined Cutter fucking me in time to the pulsing beat.

Inside the maze, Cutter led me down a small hallway with no doors on either side. He had booked the VIP room! There were only three such rooms in the entire club, each complete with a queen-size sheeted mattress, pillows, and a television bolted high on the wall, playing nonstop gay pornography. There was plenty of room to maneuver and play, unlike in the regular rooms, which were the size of broom closets, the twin-sized rubber mattress taking up half the floor space. Though thrilled to waltz into our swank accommodations, a prick of fear settled at the back of my skull. Cutter was typically a thrifty man. Why shell out the additional cash for a VIP room unless he planned something unusual, something worlds apart from our normal sexual routine?

As various unpleasant scenarios played through my fried brain, Cutter tossed his gym bag on the bed and began to strip.

"You notice anyone promising, boy?"

"I wasn't really looking."

"Well, hurry up and get undressed. We've gotta get your ass plowed."

I tried to laugh but instead produced a strange, sickly sound. The grim reality that within minutes some strange man would be ramming his cock up my ass made me feel tired and slow, like expired gelatin. I didn't want to be here. What if there were no attractive men? What if Cutter left the bathhouse disappointed? What would that do to the rest of our weekend?

"You been working out more?" Cutter asked, glancing at my naked torso.

"About the same."

"Your biceps look bigger. Your abs are getting more defined. Keep up the good work."

I rubbed my hand over my taut abdomen, checking to see if Cutter was correct. "My trainer said it would take a while to see results."

Cutter, wrapping his white towel around his waist, approached me and pulled me into an embrace. "You're a very sexy boy, Darren Young." He said that with such burnt-ember huskiness and sincerity, I knew I'd agree to whatever he requested that afternoon. I had friends who yearned to hear such grand compliments. Yes, I was a lucky boy.

"You should find someone in no time," Cutter whispered into my ear.

I finished with my clothes and wrapped the towel around my waist. I was tempted to haggle for a little more tweak, but I didn't want to make Cutter mad or delay his plans. He put such effort into these trips; I didn't want to appear ungrateful.

"Will you leave the door open for me?" I asked.

"I'll leave it cracked so if a guy wants to join me, I can wave him in."

"You mean we might wind up with a foursome?"

"The day is quite young, my boy."

I giggled, felt foolish, then left the room. As instructed, I left the door cracked so any passing man could glimpse Cutter stroking his stiffening cock. After shaking my shoulders to loosen up, I looked down each direction of the hall, wondering which to take. One led back to the maze's entrance, the other into the depths of the rooms. I had yet to pass any man in the hall. I chose to venture farther into the maze. The high floodlights dimmed as I progressed until finally that hallway opened up into a wider hall, this one with closed doors on each side all in a row. Actually, not all were closed. I passed one room with the door cracked open. Inside, a young black man stroked his cock, watching with stern concentration his organ pulse. He never noticed me. I turned away. Cutter and I had an agreement: white men only.

A moment later, a young couple passed, their heads tilted toward one another as if exchanging military code. They were my age, and one of them—the brunet—was very hot. A lithe, long body. Mouth like an open cut in the skin. Both boys glanced at me, and I recognized the haughtiness of their glares. They were undoubtedly members of what I called the Dallas Gay Mafia. You ran into these men everywhere in the city. Always dressed impeccably, gym-toned bodies, beautiful, unblemished faces. They had the leisure of condemning anyone less fantastic with a sneer. Even me. And I knew I wasn't unattractive. I looked at myself in the bathroom mirror at Cutter's house every time before leaving for the bathhouse, as if my appearance might have turned ugly overnight. Despite my confidence, these Mafia boys carried with them the ability to make me or any other man feel worthless in an instant. I looked away as I passed them. One laughed as they continued down the hall. His boyfriend halfheartedly tried to shush him before beginning to laugh, himself. Cutter wasn't fond of twinks, anyway.

When searching for men, it was customary to simply circle the hallways over and over until you found one. There were so many men leaving rooms, returning from the showers or wherever, a constant influx of new faces was at one's disposal. I passed an older man, maybe forty-five, with a beer belly and graying body hair pelting his shoulders. I passed a scrawny Mexican kid who flashed me a gold-toothed smile that I did my best to dodge. There was a trio of men, each around thirty, in heated, hushed discussion, none of them gazing at me as I walked by. How long would I have to circle these halls? Some days, some nights, it could take at least fifteen minutes. I wondered whether anyone had tried to enter our VIP room, taking up Cutter on his open-door invite. He might be fucking a guy right now, right now as these strange men either passed by unaware or sneered at me. I decided to leave the halls, try my luck elsewhere.

The hot tub was a brown-tiled in-ground pool with rushing jets placed along the walls, bubbling the water, which was usually only lukewarm. That day was no exception. I slipped off my towel, noticed with gratitude that my cock hung thick and long between my legs, and entered the water. Three other men were in the pool, but my eyes immediately locked on just one.

He sat at the opposite end, absently waving his arms through the bubbles. He was perhaps thirty; long dirty-blond hair down to his jawline; a wide, welcoming smile that seemed in response to a secret joke. I began to feel awkward staring for so long, but the man broke from his reverie and met my gaze. My god, such a smile!

"You're cute," I said. I'd learned excessive wit was just wasted breath.

"So are you."

"How long you been here?"

"Oh, I dunno. Maybe two hours."

I moved closer, the warm water thick around my surging body. The man did not draw away from my approach.

I said, in a lower voice, "You been partying?"

"Maybe. Why? You got some more?"

"I never come here without it," I said with a gravity I hoped he didn't notice.

"Is it just you here? You come with a friend?"

"My boyfriend," I said, affecting a shyness Cutter had encouraged me to employ at this point in the seduction. "His name is Cutter."

"What I wanna know is your name," the man replied, hesitantly pressing his palm against my chest.

"Darren," I said.

"I'm Raymond. So, your boyfriend likes threesomes?"

"Actually, he's more into watching hot guys fuck my ass."

"Oh, I see," he said, his smile never fading. His eyes narrowed. "And what does he do? You know, while I'm pounding your ass?"

"He takes pictures."

"You mean, for a website?"

"Oh, no, no, no. Just for our personal use." And then I

volunteered something I hadn't planned: "I think he jacks off to them when I'm not around."

Raymond's head rocked back, him howling. I hadn't believed it that funny, but I laughed too—just as Cutter had taught me.

"We're staying in one of the VIP rooms," I said. "You ever been inside one?"

"Once, a few months ago. I got roped into some orgy. It was pretty hot."

"You ready to get outta here?" I asked, backing slowly toward the hot tub's tile edge. Raymond followed me, the two of us moving like figures in a time-lapse photo.

"Hope I live up to your boyfriend's expectations," he said.

"Oh, you'll like Cutter. He just sits back and enjoys the show."

Raymond and I spoke no more as we made our way to the VIP room. When I reached the doorway, I found the door still cracked open. Carefully, I eased it farther away from the doorframe. Cutter had dimmed the lights, so it took me a moment to make out his figure on the bed, him stroking his cock while moans from the television filled the room.

"Looks like he may be busy," Raymond muttered.

"He's just waiting for us," I replied in an equally quiet tone. Then, louder, I said, "I brought company!"

Cutter bolted upright, released his cock, which bobbed in the air above his outstretched thighs. He smiled. Whether it was meant exclusively for me or for both of us, I couldn't tell.

"Did Darren tell you about me?" Cutter asked, rising from the bed. He didn't bother with the towel. He extended his hand to Raymond.

"Didn't tell me how hot you'd be."

"I'm not the main attraction," Cutter said.

"Where you want us to start?" Raymond asked, blithely

tossing his white towel onto the stone gray floor.

"Just kiss him at first," my boyfriend instructed. "Move slowly."

Raymond theatrically slapped his hands together. He then slid them around my waist and gently pulled me toward him. "I can go slow," he murmured, more for me than Cutter.

He kissed me. Every time a new man kissed me, I compared his kiss to Cutter's. The strangers' kisses were rarely better, but Raymond knew how to flutter his thick, plump lips effortlessly over my mouth. After a few moments of that, I felt the tip of his tongue push its way through my still-closed lips. I allowed it inside me. Our kiss deepened. Cutter watched in silence. As my head teetered back and forth under the force of the kiss, I caught a cockeyed glance at my boyfriend. He stood motionless, his digital camera dangling from his hand. This was unusual. Typically, Cutter could hardly wait to begin taking shots. The sudden worry pulled me away from Raymond's commanding kiss, but Raymond didn't seem to notice. Finally, Cutter snapped out of his daze and aimed the lens at Raymond and me. He snapped several shots in a row, never changing position. Raymond's hands grew bolder, one grabbing my ass, the other massaging my crotch. I still wore the towel around my hips. Through the fabric, Raymond's thick, erect cock nudged me.

"Darren," Cutter called, his voice soft. Raymond wouldn't stop kissing me. Finally, I broke free of him.

"What?" I asked, breathless.

"Suck his cock."

"Now?"

"Yeah, man. I wanna see that shit right *now*."

"What happened to going slow?" Raymond asked, more amused than disappointed.

"I just wanna watch my boy suck that huge cock of yours."

"Sounds fine to me," Raymond said. He added in a softer voice, "If that's all right with you, buddy."

Raymond was a handsome man. His face had yet to register the smile lines and slight crow's feet that Cutter's face held. There was a small gap between his two front teeth. I noticed that he instinctively bowed his head whenever he smiled. His eyes were a dazzling cornflower blue. Cutter's were merely a sad, sterile gray.

"Sure," I finally replied, easing down to my knees. "I wanna suck this cock." And with that, I slid the meaty organ between my lips, allowing it to surge into my mouth all the way to the back of my throat. I began bobbing my head, oddly enough in sync with the rhythmic moans of the porn actors onscreen. Raymond's moans filled the VIP room.

"Good boy," muttered Cutter, raising the camera to his face. "That's a good boy."

Raymond's dick tasted fantastic. I felt the wild charge I always felt knowing I could bring a man that intense a pleasure. You could go mad with the power. And there was my boyfriend, the man I loved, clicking away with his camera.

I recalled the first time Cutter showed me the photos of a bathhouse encounter. He sequenced them out over the bedspread, beaming like a proud father. "You look hot in that one, boy," he said. And then, "I thought he was going to scream when you moved your ass like that." And then, "I'm gonna have to watch you close, or you'll run off to the porn studio." I felt nothing looking at these graphic images. Because of the tweak, I rarely remembered performing any of these acts, but I played along, mimicking bashfulness or sneaky pride, whatever reaction Cutter wanted. I knew, for him, this part was just as important as the fucking itself, if not more so. He urged me to keep a snapshot or two, but I always declined. These were for him, I said, and he believed me.

Back in the VIP room, while Raymond gently thrust his hips, sending his cock deeper down my throat, I heard a man wail in the distance. I thought at first it had to be the porn, but this sounded more like a cry of anguish. Also, it definitely came from just outside the closed door. Neither Raymond nor Cutter made any movement to indicate they had heard it too, so I resumed sucking. But then the same cry, only louder.

"What the fuck was that?" Cutter asked.

We heard it again, this time trailing off into a series of jagged sobs.

Even Raymond broke from his bliss and said, "Is some guy out there crying?"

I stopped sucking his cock and turned to face the door. Cutter crossed the room and opened the door. From my position on the floor, I couldn't see what the other two saw. But then, a young man staggered through the doorway and instantly fell to his knees before us. His thin, bony shoulders shook. His arms wrapped around his narrow chest. His face contorted in bereavement. While Cutter stood still in front of the crying man, our intruder sobbed and sobbed.

Finally, Raymond spoke. "Dude, what the fuck happened?"

The crying man stopped and tried to speak, but no words came. Milky snot ran from his nose and over his lips, glistening in the dim light. He tried to speak again but could not.

Cutter gently placed a hand on his shoulder. "Are you here with someone?" he asked, showing a compassion that surprised me, though I don't know why it did. Cutter was, of course, the model of kindness. I surely knew that. "Is there someone we can get?"

The crying man settled down, sank onto the floor, bottom

resting on the soles of his feet. He wore only the expected white towel around his hips.

"I'm with Jerry," he moaned.

"Is that your boyfriend?" Cutter asked.

"I don't think so," the man stammered. "At least, not anymore!" And with that, he began to howl. I tore my gaze away from this human catastrophe to check on Raymond. It disturbed me to see his features darken, his once-ample mouth shut tightly, the lips thin and severe. He glared at the poor man through slit eyelids. His arms crossed tightly across his chest. I turned my attention back to Cutter and the crying man. Cutter tried to help the man to his feet.

"Let's go find Jerry," Cutter said.

"He doesn't want me anymore."

"I'm sure that's not true. C'mon, let's go."

"No! No! It *is* true! He found some young piece of ass in the hot tub, and that was the end of Keith."

"That's your name?" Cutter asked. "Keith?"

Keith moaned and nodded. He dabbed furiously at his eyes. By then, Cutter had managed to maneuver the intruder back toward the doorway. Believing the situation would soon resolve, I returned my attention to Raymond only to find him grabbing his towel from the floor. The brisk, violent strokes he made wrapping it around his waist distressed me.

"You don't have to leave," I said.

"Sorry, man, that was kind of a buzzkill."

"My boyfriend's taking care of it."

Raymond stomped through the door. Cutter and the crying man had already gone outside. I stood there, helpless. I wondered if any of the pictures Cutter had taken were angled highly enough to capture Raymond's lovely face. More likely, they were centered solely on my lips around his cock. After all, that's what my boyfriend wanted to remember: how I looked giving another man pleasure as I would for him soon after.

The door clicked shut behind Raymond. I glanced down and saw my swollen cock begin its retreat beneath the towel's fabric. This flood of disappointment surprised me. Of course, there were other candidates stalking the halls right now. All I had to do was wait for Cutter to return, then leave to find one. As much as I always dreaded our trips here, when the pursuit was in full bloom, I allowed myself to get carried away on the adrenaline rush. Still, I needed something to numb myself a little further, to guarantee no doubts would descend when I resumed the hunt. I hurried to the side of the bed and found Cutter's gym bag. I riffled through it, looking for the bag of tweak. Just a couple of hits, that's all I needed. After locating the pipe wrapped inside a sock, I loaded it with a sizable crystal only to realize I'd yet to locate a lighter. I ransacked the bag once again, but this time had no luck. Could Cutter have forgotten? Or was this his passive-aggressive way of controlling the amount of tweak I smoked. He worried about how much I smoked. Defeated, I sank onto the bed and listlessly watched the screen as one man penetrated another man's bobbing ass. The two men moved with the certain rhythm of a charging locomotive, and I couldn't help but wonder whether Raymond and I would have moved with comparable precision.

After a few more moments of watching the men fuck, I slid off the bed, tucked the loaded pipe back into the gym bag and made my way for the door. Even though being alone in the VIP room meant I was spared the ravenous or dismissive glares of the strange men outside, it also meant I had no one to distract me from the sense of rot and doom I felt in this impersonal fuck factory. Just a month ago, I'd spent the night with a man I met while at my cousin's wedding in Tyler. He was big and charming and insatiable in bed. I managed to forget, at least for a few moments, that Cutter was back in Dallas waiting for me. What would I do if one day Cutter asked me to do something I simply couldn't face? Would I lose him? Would he leave me stranded in some rented room with damp sheets and faded semen stains on the walls?

"My god, some people are so fucking needy!" Cutter declared as he burst through the door. He crossed the room with long, energetic strides.

"What took so long?"

"He wouldn't stop crying."

"Did you ever find his boyfriend?"

"I asked his room number, but the guy flat-out refused to go back there. I asked him where he wanted to go instead. You won't believe what happened then."

The two men in the porn playing above increased their volume and urgency. Cutter shook his head and smacked his forehead with an open palm.

"Anyway," he said, "we're standing near the hot tub and he just comes out and grabs my dick, says he wants only me to fuck him. Said we could rent a separate room, his treat."

"Oh, my god," I said with no affect. It was always painful to be reminded of this: Cutter was a devastating man. Of course, other men desired him. And there was no guarantee they'd desire me too.

"I just looked at him and said—and you should've heard how I said it. I looked him dead in the eye and said, 'I have a boyfriend, you dumb faggot.'" Making that declaration, he sounded like a no-nonsense sheriff from an old sitcom.

"What did he say?" I asked, rising to my knees on the bed.

"That's even funnier. He just shrugged, shook his head and said, 'Your loss.' Then he walked into the sauna. I guess he's still looking for dick."

"What a loser!" I cried.

"No shit. Maybe we shouldn't have come here today."

I couldn't keep the enthusiasm out of my tone. "You mean you're ready to leave?"

Cutter rounded the bed and stopped, facing me. I was still on my knees atop the mattress so our heads were on the same level. He reached out and softly caressed my cheek. He held my gaze for so long, I forgot entirely about Raymond's electric blue eyes. Yes, there were other desirable men in the world, in this very building, but Cutter Drake had chosen me. Me. And whatever I had to endure to keep his love would be done to perfection.

"I'd hate the VIP room to go to waste," he purred.

"Should we leave the door open?"

"Nah, let's leave it shut. I don't feel like sharing you right now."

"You mean that?"

He kissed me briefly, haltingly on my lips. "I'd never lie to you, boy."

He fucked me until I was exhausted and sweating like a sow in the mid-August sun. Afterward I lay beside him, the sheets askew from our thrashing. For that blessed moment, I listened to Cutter's breath, slowed mine till it fell into rhythm with his. It took me a bit to realize he'd spoken.

"You wanna run outside and grab me a water?" he asked.

"Don't you have Gatorade in your bag?"

"Yeah, but water sounds better."

"I'm so fucking whipped right now," I moaned.

"Please."

"Just drink your Gatorade."

"I'll suck your dick if you go," Cutter said.

I rose to my side and looked down at him, hoping he could see the merriment in my gaze. "You should do that because you love me."

"I'll love you more when I'm hydrated."

"Okay."

Relieved that Cutter hadn't asked me to leave the door ajar, I carried a limp dollar in my fist for the drink machine. More than anything, I wished I could make the trek to the lobby without passing any other man. I was done with men for that day, every man except Cutter. I turned the corner and headed out of the maze.

I only saw two men in the hot tub and another three watching the lounge television as I hurried past. None of them noticed me. I slid the dollar into the drink machine and pushed the correct button. Just as I bent over to retrieve the bottle from the machine, a figure in a white towel appeared suddenly at my side.

"You better be grateful he loves you," the figure said.

Alarmed, my breath caught, I twisted my head over my shoulder and saw Keith glaring at me. His eyes were still red and bleary.

"What did you say to me?"

"You heard me the first time."

I gulped then spit out, "Cutter told me what you did."

Keith's stance softened. He hitched up one shoulder in defiance. "Can't blame me for trying. You know how hot he is—you're the one fucking him."

"I have to get back to the room," I stammered and abruptly turned to leave. Keith followed me, his wide strides matching my own.

"You think some kid can keep him happy for long?"

"Stop following me!" One of the men watching television turned to see the commotion.

"If he really wanted just you, he wouldn't take you to this place."

"I don't wanna talk to you."

"I'll keep an eye out for him, I promise you that." We had reached the windowed hallway connecting the lounge to the maze. Keith seized my shoulder, spun me around so I faced him. I couldn't remember the last time a man looked at me with such hate, and I knew in that moment he wished me dead.

"I'm not giving up, kid," he said. "Men like him get bored with little boys and they come looking for me. Just remember that."

I nodded dumbly and backed away. I bumped into a wrought-iron table, jumped at the sudden screech the table leg made across the floor. Recovering, I ran into the maze of rented rooms, fully expecting Keith to follow me. But after I reached the hallway leading to our VIP room, he was gone. Taking a moment to collect myself before joining Cutter—I couldn't tell him, never!—I felt hot, stinging tears in the corners of my eyes. I wiped them away roughly. Taking a deep breath, I turned the doorknob.

"What took you so long, boy?"

"There was more than one brand of water," I said.

"Don't fall for that bullshit. I don't care what label's on the bottle, water is fucking water."

"Here you go," I said, handing him the drink. He grabbed it and unscrewed the lid. Knowing I was giving myself away, I glared at my boyfriend as if trying to memorize his face before he disappeared forever.

"Boy, what's wrong?"

"Are you ready to go, baby?"

"Don't you want me to suck your dick?"

"I don't care. I just wanna go!"

I felt the tears slide down my cheeks. I buried my face in my hands. The shakes my body made as I cried left no doubt that I needed my boyfriend's comfort—right now.

Cutter took me into his arms. "Baby, it's all right. I didn't know this place upset you that much."

"It does, it does."

"C'mon, boy, you're not supposed to cry in a bathhouse."

"What *can* you do here?"

My boyfriend, the man I loved, smiled. "This," he said, and pressed his mouth over mine. And with that, I was silenced once again. Through the speakers suspended over the room, an insistent bass line pounded. The boys on television groaned and grunted. Cutter pulled his face away. He gazed into my eyes. Did he want me to do something? I couldn't remember the last time I'd seen that look on his face. I smiled and hoped I'd soon recall what that devastating gaze meant for my happiness, the happiness I felt pleasing the man I loved.

THE VALDETIAN

Mark Wildyr

I lay panting as my companion crawled off of me and strode into the bathroom. Stretching lazily on the bed, I waited to witness one of the most marvelous transformations on God's green earth. Ajax Froman had entered the shower a handsome, virile, sexually sated adult; he would emerge as a fetching, loose-limbed nineteen-year-old adolescent in baggy clothes trailing an air of naïve innocence. The amazing thing was that both images were accurate. At times, he seemed downright otherworldly...for lack of a better term. He was an incredible fucking machine packaged in a slender, lightly sculpted body who considered an intimate relationship with another male to be no big deal. Nonetheless, he had thus far honored my request to guard our secret from the rest of the world.

"Hey, man." Jax gave me a crooked smile as he returned to the room running long, tapered fingers through dark-brown locks that curled when damp. "That was awesome. I dig doing it with you."

"Right back at you." I adopted his patois. "I dig that big, swinging dick you sport, sport."

Jax beamed like he was lit up by neon. "You like it, huh?"

"Sure do, my man. But I can't keep from wondering who else gets a helping of it."

"Nobody. I kinda like to stick with one guy until it's time to move on."

That sent a spasm of alarm through me. "Anybody else on the horizon?"

"Naw." He shifted into a more comfortable slouch. "Well, there's this jock at school. He's been sniffing around. Think he might be about to make his move."

I sat up abruptly and tried to hide my fright. "A jock? Didn't know you went for that type."

He gave a characteristic shrug that was so sexy I started tingling. The scent of soap and body lotion assailed me. "Don't usually, but this guy's hands-down hunky. The kind you get wet dreams about. Only problem is, he probably sees himself as a top, too."

"He know about you?"

"Naw. He's just...attracted, I guess you'd say."

Jax went through his usual pat down, checking pockets for keys, wallet and whatever else he carried in his camo pants. "Gotta go, babe." He leaned down for a kiss. Jax was a kisser. Learned it from movies and TV, I expect. And he'd learned damned well. The taste of his full lips almost rekindled my fire.

"When can I see you again?" I asked as he pulled away. "Next week?"

"Can't. Got midterms. Be studying or taking tests all week. How about the week after?"

"Fine, so long as you don't find time to squeeze in that jock."

"Robert? Naw. Don't think so. Probably won't happen for a while."

As usual, I suffered withdrawal symptoms the moment the door closed behind his trim butt. The beautiful kid had really gotten to me after only three sessions, the first of which was purely platonic. To fight my "post-Ajax depression," I got busy around the house. At the top of the list was the front lawn, assuming I had enough strength to follow a mower around the yard, which was problematic. The sun was almost down, so perhaps the twilight air would revive me.

As I headed for the garage door on uncertain legs, the phone rang. At least I thought it did; the tone was weak and off-key. I picked up the receiver and answered. There was silence for a moment, but as I started to hang up, a wracking rattle that could have been a breath came over the wire.

"H...hello?" I said uncertainly.

"That boy...he fucked you good. Really good."

As shocked as I was, I managed to notice the voice was strange—metallic, yet with intelligent inflections. It had to be someone playing tricks with one of those voice-altering devices. I grinned broadly.

"Ajax? Is that you? I've already admitted that you fuck like a rabbit!"

"A-jax. He is a beautiful human being, is he not? And he has a big appendage. Much bigger than yours."

"You don't have to fish for compliments, you good-looking son of a bitch. You come on back, and I'll show you how beautiful and manly you are. And, yeah, you've got a big sausage." Silence. "Ajax? Are you there?"

"The handsome A-jax, he is not here," that odd voice replied.

Angered and fearful that I was being outed, I gripped the

phone and made my voice harsh. "Who is this? Answer me! Who's on the phone?"

Silence, and then a noise that could have been laughter, although it sounded like no laughter I knew. "This is your phone speaking."

"Yeah, yeah! Who is this? If this isn't Ajax, how did you know about him? What's going on here?"

"I know about A-jax because I watched him perform his fantastic sex act upon you. He does it so gracefully and so forcefully."

"You what? Impossible! We were in a—" I swallowed my tongue.

"Yes, in a closed room. But I watched nonetheless. It is a pity he can perform only for such a short time. He is a great pleasure to watch."

"Such a short time? The kid fucked me for better than thirty minutes!" Oh, shit! I'd admitted it aloud. Yes, but to whom had I confessed? Someone from work? From the law firm where I'd practiced for the past three years? "Who is this? You fucker, tell me who you are!"

Silence for a long moment. "You would not understand."

"What's to understand? Just tell me who you are so I can sue your ass to hell and gone for invasion of privacy."

A crackle of static came out of the receiver, and somehow I understood it was a sigh. "I am from far away, a place you will not know."

This joker spun a good tale, but he wasn't perfect. As he talked, his voice lost some of its tinniness, sounding more normal. "Try me. I'm a pretty at geography."

"Geography will not help you. I am a Valdetian."

"Where the fuck is that? And what's your name?"

"Far away." The voice took on a note of resignation. "Beyond reach. And my name would be unpronounceable to you. You may call me Valdetian."

"Where are you?" I started going into my lawyer's deposition mode.

"All around you."

My back puckered as I scanned the room. I was alone. "Bullshit!" I lost some of my professional cool. "Cut the crap and come out where I can see you!" The hair on my arms stood up.

"You are not ready yet. I am not like you."

"Then what are you like?" My skin crawled. My eyes searched the room, and I wished that I had turned on the lights. It was coming up on dark, and the vanity lights from the bathroom Ajax had left burning only half-relieved the gloom.

Another silence, and then, "Like this house."

"My house? My fucking house is talking to me? I'm supposed to call my house Valdetian?"

"I am not your house. I merely...utilize it."

"You're not making any sense."

"I warned that you would not understand. Perhaps this will make it clearer. I have two forms; my own, and this house."

"Where in the house?" I grabbed the question out of the air. Was I going crazy or was this was really happening?

"Everywhere. I can abandon my own shape to shelter in an inanimate environment when danger threatens."

I snorted...actually snorted. "Come on!" My turn to pause. "This Valdetia, is it in Europe or Asia? Or maybe Africa?"

"My home is Valdetia. I am Valdetian. Like your home is America, and you are—"

"Yeah, yeah! I get it. Look, fella. I'm a reasonably intelligent man...for a lawyer, that is. You don't expect me to really believe—"

"Hang up the telephone," the voice ordered so sternly that I instantly obeyed. "You see," my grandfather clock said to me, "we do not need an instrument of communication to communicate."

I about jumped out of my skin. "Get outta here!" I was reduced to street talk.

"I have," the mirror over the mantel said. "Many times at night I leave when no one is stirring. But I always return."

"Why? Why my house?"

"Your neighbors have families. You live alone. And your lifestyle is more interesting. Most of the men here consort with *Mektosas*...what you call women or females. You prefer *Meksos*, as do I."

"You're a homo Valdetian?" At that point I knew I was taking this semi-seriously.

"Homo? That is not a word I am familiar with. Much of what I know, I learned in this house, and that is not a word you commonly use."

"How about queer or gay?"

"Ah. The preference for one of your own *clete*. Your own sex. Also, you play with your thing...I believe you call it a dick. A-jax calls it a cock. I think I prefer A-jax's word."

I'm sure the soles of my feet blushed. "You've been spying on me!"

"Of course. How else can I learn? I like the way you close your eyes when you near your time. Your mouth opens, and you let out this strange sound."

My ears went red.

"A-jax closes his eyes, too, when he approaches ejaculation. You are a handsome man, Rex, but forgive me; A-jax is far superior."

"No argument from me," I mumbled, glad to get off of the

subject of masturbation. "You see everything that goes on in here?"

Silence. Then, "Yes."

"No, you don't!" I exclaimed, suddenly understanding something. "You have to have eyes to see. Like the mirror or the TV. Right?"

"But I hear everything."

"You son of a bitch! I'll fix you. I'll take down all the mirrors and move the TV out of my bedroom. I'll blind you, you bastard."

"Do you not like to be watched?"

Taking a mental step backward, I snapped, "I'll get back to you on that. Right now I'm going to find the hidden cameras and microphones you jokers installed in here. Then I'm calling the cops."

My uninvited guest remained mute as I turned on every light and scoured the entire house for two solid hours. I came up with nothing. No small, innocuous cameras, no miniature plastic bugs. Nothing. Finally, I collapsed on the sofa, mentally exhausted.

"Satisfied?" the glass on my coffee table asked, almost scaring me to death.

"I can't get my head around this. Go on, convince me."

"Shall I tell you how you awaken every morning with your cock erect?"

"Piss hard," I mumbled defensively.

"Or how you come home some nights and sprawl on the sofa to finger your thing through your clothing. Sometimes, that is enough, but sometimes, you take it out and massage it until your fluid spurts out. You have not done that since you brought the amazing A-jax home. Tell me, why do you not bring other young men home with you? Only A-jax comes to your house."

"Ajax!" I shouted inanely. "It's Ajax; not A-jax."

"Thank you. I will remember. Tell me how you met our beautiful friend."

So I told the coffee mug on my lamp table how one Saturday three weeks ago, I'd given an incredibly handsome, graceful and overwhelmingly sensual teenaged hitchhiker a lift to UNM on East Central. The kid was so breathtaking I was loath to let him go, so I offered to buy lunch. He not only accepted; he talked a leg off me, something I was not accustomed to from the teens of my acquaintance. He was an American lit major in his sophomore year. His old buggy was on the fritz but should be repaired early the next week.

We ended up killing the afternoon, and the more I got to know him, the stronger the sexual attraction became. When I took him back to the university, I knew we'd meet again and probably end up in bed.

That cataclysmic event came a week later. It appeared to be a chance meeting, but in reality, our vibes the previous weekend had set a date in stone for the same time, same place the next Saturday. He bailed out of a vintage Chevy and got in my BMW, flashing the brilliant smile I found so endearing. Twenty minutes later, I was lying in my own bed getting the fucking of my life.

"Jax is a natural; unusually skilled for one of his tender years," I finished.

"How does it become Jax instead of Ajax?"

"A nickname, a familiar. Makes him into a friend, an intimate."

"I see. And what is your theory as to how Jax became so skilled?"

"As I say, part of it is natural ability. But he grew up on a Montana ranch watching the animals do it. And he told me he bedded cowboys from horizon to horizon in the Big Sky Country, starting at an early age." I laughed. "Most kids are just beginning to jerk off by then. He was already fucking. Today was our second sexual bout, and it was as fantastic as the first."

"Call him back. I should like to observe him again. And you, too, of course. You are quite attractive as you squirm beneath him. I notice that you use two positions. In one, you face him; in the other he enters you from behind."

"I like the first." What was this squirrelly satisfaction I got from discussing Ajax's bedroom gymnastics with my TV, my mantel, the light fixture, even the ashtray? "Because I can watch him do it to me. But the other way is good, too, because it's full-body contact."

"He prefers that, I believe," my reading lamp suggested.

"Yes, I think you are right."

"Contact him," the voice, which was beginning to sound a bit like me, urged again.

"Can't. He drove his own car today and won't be back at the dorm yet. And you heard him tell me he has to study for midterm exams."

"Tomorrow is what you call Sun-day. Try him tomorrow. Lure him back!" one of the tiny mirrors sewn into the avant-garde throw pillow on my lap insisted. I hastily threw it aside.

"We'll see," I hedged in the face of such intensity and fled outside to cut the lawn in the dark, wondering at every step if the Valdetian rode the mower with its dangerous whirling blades.

After a restless night of listening for—and hearing—rustling noises in the dark, creaks from the attic, and a thud in the kitchen, I rose and staggered naked into the bathroom looking like a wreck. I pissed, rinsed my hands, and doused my face in cold water before clearing away my eyes with a towel. Something in the mirror did not look right; it was cloudy. Vainly, I tried to wash off what I took to be soap film. At length, I stood back and regarded it for what it was.

"I see you, Valdetian."

"No," my mirror answered quietly. "You see only the roiling of my discontent. You shall not see the true me until it is time."

"And when will that be?"

"When I deem you ready."

"Let me be the judge of that. Why are you here, anyway? Your spaceship crash, or something?"

"Valdetians have progressed far beyond such archaic craft. However, you are correct in assuming that something went awry with my mode of transportation."

"So now you're stuck here in my house? How long have you been here?"

"Two of your months. Long enough to know you live a life of quiet desperation."

"What are you talking about? I'm a lawyer! I make good money. The hours are not bad. I work out at the gym and am healthy. I'm passing good looking and have a decent body. Lots of people envy me."

"Then why were you alone until Ajax came into your life?"

"I wasn't alone. I had relationships. I just didn't bring any of them home. Until Jax."

"Yes. He is worth bringing home. Call him."

"Nope. If I push him too hard, he'll get restless and hook up with that jock he mentioned. That Robert guy."

"And this is bad?"

"You heard him, Valdetian. He tends to stay monogamous

until it's time to move on. I don't want him to move on."

"But I *must* see him perform again."

"Not going to happen, Val. When he comes back, I'm covering every mirror, every television screen, the works. I want my privacy with that young man."

"When he comes, I will watch. In the meantime, I enjoy seeing you like this."

So help me, when I realized my mirror was staring at my naked body, I started to get hard.

"Ah, that is nice. Manipulate yourself for me."

I wet my lips and started to tell him to fuck off. But my hands pressed against my thighs and then cupped my balls. It was pleasant knowing someone...or something...was watching. I grasped my now hard cock in my right hand and tugged on it a couple of times. My nipples tingled. My back rippled. Before I knew it, I was masturbating seriously.

"Yes, yes! That is almost as good as watching Ajax fuck you. Do it, Rex. Make it come."

I increased the rhythm as my testicles started to draw up. I leaned forward against the countertop, thrusting my groin toward the mirror. A moment later, I exploded. My cum shot all over the glass. I panted and relaxed as sperm oozed through my fingers.

"Beautiful! Beautiful. Do it again."

"Are you fucking crazy?" I wheezed. "Give a guy a break."

Nonetheless, my butt continued to prickle as I showered and shaved. I finished dressing in my bedroom, keenly aware that I was under observation. I faced my dresser and grasped my basket, shaking it at the mirror before starting for the garage. As I reached the kitchen, my toaster asked where I was going.

"Few chores. Gotta get some groceries. Won't be long.

Unless I spot a buff kid with a nice ass. Enjoy the house; it's all yours."

"When will you return?"

"Couple of hours. You're free to roam until then."

After my tasks were done, I played cat and mouse with a kid with a cute bubble butt at the Albuquerque library for damned near an hour before some of his buddies showed up and swept him away, ruining what I think was a mutual desire for me to bury my cock between those nice buns. Following that, I had a cup of espresso at Starbucks and took a walk-through of an antique shop. Finally, I admitted I was dawdling, avoiding a return to my alien-infested home. What the hell was I going to do about that short of burning the place down? Did Terminix handle space mice?

Might as well face the music; or more to the point, the Valdetian. When I inserted my key in the lock, my peephole almost made me pee my pants.

"Where have you been? Hurry up and get in here."

"What's the hurry? And stop scaring me like that. Twenty-seven's too young for white hair."

"What is the hurry? It is our beautiful friend, Ajax."

"What about him?" Comprehension dawned. "You didn't! Please tell me you didn't call him. How did you even get his telephone number?"

"You thoughtfully left it in the telephone, properly labeled Ajax Froman. Yes, I dialed his number, and he thought it was you," my own voice said from somewhere down the hall.

I began to get a bad feeling. "What the hell did you say to him?"

"He claimed he was too busy studying, so I suggested he bring along his new friend, Robert."

"What?" I roared. "Don't encourage him, Valdetian. He'll crawl aboard that kid and forget all about me."

The voice, this time coming from the computer screen in my home office, took on that tinny quality again, and I understood Val was disturbed. "I offered to join them. That is, I offered for you to join them. I suggested they could both fuck you and end this problem of being tops, which I understand means they both wish to fuck rather than be fucked."

"Oh, shit!" I moaned. "And what did he say to that?"

"He seemed somewhat offended. Ajax said he did not go for threesomes."

"You've fucked it all up. The kid will never see me again!"

"To the contrary. Ajax is on his way over here right this minute."

"With Robert? How did you manage that?"

"I, speaking as you, of course, offered the use of your bedroom and assured him the front door would be unlocked. I...*you* promised to remain closeted in your office until he left."

I collapsed in my chair, devastated. This...this *creature* had screwed up my life just so he could watch Ajax perform in bed, and there was nothing I could do about it short of heading the kid off at the door and alienating him forever. The front doorbell rang, bringing me out of the chair.

"Do not answer it," the computer warned. "He said he would ring the bell to reassure his companion no one was home."

Moments later, I heard the rumble of nervous male laughter in my front hallway. I clasped my head in my hands and suffered in silence.

After a few minutes, the creature spoke. "Look."

I raised my head and gazed into my computer screen. Ajax... my beautiful Ajax...held a sturdy, handsome blond kid in his arms. Robert fought the kiss for a minute, but once Ajax found his lips, the jock surrendered. I soon lost the power to protest as I watched the most erotic striptease I'd ever witnessed. Each disrobed the other, one garment at a time. Robert's erection sent me into the stratosphere, probably someplace near Valdetia. When Jax slowly rolled a pair of bikini shorts over his own downy thighs, excitement turned to elation. That slender, tousle-headed youth of my dreams was bigger. In every way: length, thickness...sheer bulk. Robert seemed to lose some of his swagger.

"Look," Valdetian said from somewhere over my shoulder. "Ajax is more the man."

"Yes, but let's see who sticks it to whom. I'm betting on Jax, although it's gonna be a blow to the ego for that jock to take a cock up his butt."

It was a seesaw, but Ajax played it masterfully, just as he had for those Montana cowboys, I imagine. He used his full, sensuous lips to drive the jock crazy and then lured the blond into a little payback. By the time they tumbled onto the bed, Robert was on the bottom. Ajax gave him a full, deep-throat kiss while spreading the boy's legs with his own. When he cradled Robert's knees in his elbows, the jock protested. Jax stilled the rebellion with another kiss while he fingered the blond's ass. Soon he was easing that big log into Robert's channel.

After that, my handsome stud became liquid mercury, thrusting and stabbing, slow, fast, hard, languid, his hand continuously at Robert's groin, toying with his testicles, pumping his cock. Robert broke first. With a mighty shout, the jock wrapped his legs around Jax's narrow waist and lifted himself off the bed. Cum flew all over both of them. That was when Jax really got down to business. His climax was awesome.

"See," came the voice behind me. "The handsome boy closes his eyes during orgasm. And they are such beautiful eyes."

I stood suddenly, catching my erection painfully on the edge of the computer stand. "I'm going in there! I've got to have him! Now!"

"Think!" Valdetian ordered. "If you barge in on them now, Ajax will be angry. He may never return again."

"He may not anyway," I said savagely, "now that he's found another."

"Look at them closely," my computer screen ordered. "Ajax is satisfied, as he always is. Happy. He goes about cleaning up and dressing in a comfortable way. But watch the other boy."

It was true. Robert looked as if a storm cloud hovered overhead. Things had not gone as planned. I knew he had expected to seduce the slender, graceful dark-haired kid from the northern plains. He'd intended to stuff his manhood up Jax and expected the sophomore to be grateful for the privilege of taking it. Now the big athlete was confused, mortified. Afraid.

His first words confirmed my conclusions. "Let's get outta this joint before the guy who lives here comes back. You ever tell anybody about this, Froman, and I'll have your ass."

Unabashed, my beautiful lover looked him dead in the eye and ended it on the spot with an arrow to the ego. "Not like I just had yours, Robert. That'll never happen."

I could hardly contain myself until they were out of the house, and then I rushed into my bedroom to inhale the aroma of their lovemaking. Musk and tangy semen. I tore off my clothes and leaned over the bed, my erection pulsing wildly.

"It drove you mad, did it not?" Valdetian's voice came from somewhere behind me. Ignoring him, I grasped myself and began to pump. "I think you are ready," he whispered.

"R...ready?" I gasped. "For what?" I whipped my cock

desperately, strangely elated that he watched.

"For me to emerge. For you to see me as I truly am. We are not entirely compatible, my handsome earthling, but I believe that I can satisfy you," the Valdetian said over my shoulder.

I released my raging cock and turned, eager for relief, any relief!

And screamed in abject terror!

RED, RED, AND MORE RED

Doug Harrison

So, what's with my infatuation with red? A remnant of the long, sleek, bright-red fire truck I received for my fourth birthday and obsessively played with, ignoring all other toys? Or memories of my first two-wheel bicycle, and my dad patiently teaching me how to ride, bless him? Or my first car, my very own auto, a red Volkswagen Beetle?

No matter. I must mow the lawn today, after much procrastination, of course, and choose an outfit to match my red lawn tractor. My one-acre spread in Hawaii harbors a small but comfortable home, to which I have retired. I'm bounded by jungle on three sides; I can gaze into dense foliage through a large picture window in my office as I type. But the house's other walls are framed by lawn, far too much of it, an unfortunate reminder of suburban California neighborhoods where I roosted and a distinct surprise when I searched for property. Fortunately, my grassy meadow contains three large, rocky islands of contorted lava outcrops, hidey-holes for resting and nesting mongooses, variegated foliage, wild orchards and a smattering of stately Ohia trees. Why developers didn't leave most of the majestic Ohias intact remains a mystery. The Hawaiian equivalent of California redwoods that survive forest fires, Ohia trees spring almost magically from cooled lava flows; a pocket of water, an airborne seed, and poof, a tree is born. But I make the most of my stately lawn and give thanks for what Ohias I do have, delighted and proud to be their protector.

My lawn tractor is a joy to ride. Whenever I ride it, I bounce along thinking of Mr. Toad in his new red motorcar "...going merrily over, the road that leads to Dover..."

But as ever there's a short somewhere in the electrical system that no one can find, certainly not me, so I must first engage my readily accessible red battery charger.

I pass my red Camry in the carport, hook up the charger and ponder my riding outfit. Jodhpurs and riding crop are not necessary, but a cap is in order. In fact, my skin specialist has warned me not to venture into the sun without dressing like a fireman. No kidding! No skin showing! Bullshit! That's not why this sun bunny moved to Hawaii. I know I'm toying with fire, but, at my age, I don't worry about consequences. So I compromise with a red cap, no shirt, red Puma sneakers, and gobs of suntan lotion.

And I wait until late afternoon—low sun, but more traffic on our road, which could be good or bad. My proclivity for exhibitionism is occasionally overridden by propriety. I live in a development where lots range in size from one to three acres, different than the typical tract development. My property is on the main cross street, with more than the usual traffic. Who might cruise by? So, let's go fishing, not trolling, whilst we mow the lawn!

Let's see: red and white, baggy, waist-to-knee surfer shorts, red hip-to-midthigh gym shorts, red Speedos or a red thong? I prefer the thong, having been told I look good in it (who's to argue?), but that's pushing the envelope should little old ladies tootle by, or a young couple meander along with their baby stroller. I thank god mankind has evolved from the white cotton boxers and briefs of my youth to colorful, form-fitting, even form-enhancing underwear. It feels great to harbor plumage, and the demarcation between underwear and outerwear, like the boundary of a black hole, is nebulous. I settle on the red Speedos, the ones with the extra-narrow waistband, of course. I stuff myself into them, no cock ring needed, excitement propels engorgement, and the pouch is promptly filled. Of course I stretch the drawstring to its elastic limit (pun intended for you engineers), and secure it with a square knot.

Battery charged. Engine engaged. Back out of garage. And off we go!

The palm and coconut trees on my property provide some shade, but mostly I'm in direct sun. And my thong tan line shows it. Great for the nude beach, but that's another story.

I'm putt-putting about twenty yards from the street and notice a battered white flatbed truck approaching. It's towing a trailer supporting a sleek, top-of-the-line green John Deere lawn tractor. The young, shirtless Hawaiian driver decelerates and cranes his neck as he passes. He turns the corner three lots away, the motor drifts into semi-silence, and gains in volume. Must have done a U-turn, a difficult maneuver with his lengthy set of wheels. He's obviously curious, possibly intrigued, and, goddamn, perhaps serious, with the requisite skill set. It's time to mow the patch contiguous to the road.

He approaches.

I smile.

He slows.

I wave.

He waves back.

I brake and idle.

He pulls to a stop near me.

I rub my crotch.

He kills his engine and disembarks.

I stand, my crotch proudly perched on the rim of the steering wheel. Speaking of rimming... I hop off, and we stand chest to chest. He's five-nine to my six feet, with gorgeous deep-brown skin, long black hair tied into a neat ponytail with a red rubber band and sparkling black eyes, that hold who knows what memories. I should have worn the thong. Nah, let him explore, if he's so inclined. I extend my hand.

"Aloha, I'm Doug, nickname's Puma."

"Aloha, I like that," he says as his eyes raster my torso, pausing on my nipple rings, and proceeding to my runner's thighs, lingering at the elongated bulge in my Speedos and its concomitant Shmoo-shaped stain. "I'm Kalani. Means—"

"The sky," I interrupt. "Beautiful name."

He arches his eyebrows and nods. "Also means 'high chief,'" he says with a slight smirk.

"You look like a warrior," I add. "Like to see you in a native loincloth."

He grins. "It's called a malo."

"Or less," I add, returning his smile and raising the ante.

We shake. His eyes reflect his astonishment that I've mastered the Hawaiian three-grip, sliding handshake. He recovers and rubs his crotch. "Good going, bro."

"Care for a drink?" I ask, knowing full well what the answer will be.

"*Mahalo,*" he replies.

"Drive in," I say. "I'll leave the tractor here." I'm wondering how the fuck I'll start it after he leaves, hopefully after dark, perhaps in the a.m. "Stubborn battery," I mumble.

Kalani shakes his head, pulls out a set of jumper cables and repairs the tractor and my attitude.

"Follow me," I say, "lots of room to park."

We proceed along the driveway, underneath arching palm trees, and I direct him to a spot while I pull into the garage. But he parks parallel to the triple carport, blocking the entire entrance. We get out.

"Gotcha," he says. The key is almost tucked into his pocket when I sidle up to him. I have all I can do not to go down on him then and there. But I do rub his bulging crotch. Nice! Very, very nice indeed! We stare into each other's eyes.

"C'mon in," I say with a flick of my head, and grab his hand.

Mail is left in a box near the road, but parcels are delivered to the door. And I know the Fed Ex dyke would be more than tolerant, indeed would grin ear-to-ear, were she to approach in her spiffy, spankin' new, walk-in white truck. She's most proud of it, and I've admired it several times—seems they go together. We've bonded, and she views me as more than just another customer.

We sashay toward the house, arms swinging, remove our shoes and enter.

"Nice," Kalani says, looking at the four-foot-square glass etching of a plumaria blossom suspended over the counter that separates kitchen and dining room.

I utter a slow, "Thanks," as I kneel, wrap my arms around his thighs, and press my head into his crotch, savoring the aroma of sweaty Carhartts. I breathe deeply.

"Nice; very, very nice," I whisper.

Kalani runs his fingers through what little hair I have, moves his hips up and down a bit, and morphs into a circular motion as he grabs the back of my head and pushes it deeper into his crotch. I feel his hard-on, even through the thick cloth. I nibble, he thrusts, and I reach for his zipper.

"Later," he says, "I'm thirsty." He pulls me to my feet.

Shit, I think, *where're my manners*? But at least his remark is a harbinger of...of what? My head spins with possibilities.

"Lilikoi juice?" I ask. "Freshly picked and squeezed this morning."

"Sounds good. I noticed all the fruit trees you have."

I nod. We clink our glasses in a silent toast and take a few sips.

Shit, double shit, I think, my face contorted with embarrassment and frustration. *I haven't even invited him into the living room.*

He takes my drink, raises the two glasses in another silent toast, sets them on the breakfront, and steps out of his tan shorts and tighty-whities.

His dick springs forth, thwacks his abdomen, almost reaching his navel, and after a few diminishing oscillations, finds its equilibrium aimed at my crotch. I kneel, purse my lips and latch onto it while wrapping my arms around his legs. My fingernails dig into his inner thighs, he squirms and pushes his fat dick to its limit—his public hair tangles with my moustache. Many years of experience come into play and I don't gag. I grab his dickhead with my throat muscles and tease him—clench, relax, clench, relax. He hops from foot to foot and throws his head back. Then I capture his dickhead with my lips and nibble his corona—gently, harshly, gently, harshly. I'm able to tease some spit from my pursed lips, the thumb and forefinger of my right hand form a circle that I coat and slide along his shaft—back and forth, back and forth in sync with my lip motions.

"Mother fucker!" he yells. "I'm gonna come."

"Not yet," I say as I lean back on my haunches and form an evil grin, watching him pant and clench his fists. I stare at his bobbing cock, glistening with precum.

He reaches for his dick and I swat his hand. I lick his piss slit and capture a large silky drop before it can slither to the edge and float to the rug.

"Your turn," he says, and tugs at my Speedos. They don't move. I untie my drawstring with a flourish and stand stone-statue still. He chuckles and guides my briefs to my ankles. My saber springs forth, almost a challenge.

"Let's go outside," I suggest. Or was it a command?

"But, but..." he stammers.

"It's an acre lot, the backyard is deep and surrounded by jungle on three sides. Takes a machete to get through it. We'll be alone. I promise."

"Well, okay." He tries to cover his dick with his hands.

"Relax," I order, "and help me."

He follows me into the bathroom and notices my floggers hanging from a rack as we pass my office. He pauses but says nothing. We enter the bathroom and stop short.

"What's that?" he asks.

"A fuck bench," I reply.

"I should've guessed. What're those slots for?"

"Straps, to secure the willing victim."

"Oh."

He stares at the wooden contraption. Its two angled sides are trapezoidal in shape, three feet long on the floor, two feet across at the top. The rear edges are thirty inches tall; the front, thirty-three inches tall. They support a sloped leather pad, thirty-three inches long, six inches wide. Hinges screwed into a cross piece near the floor separate the side pieces and provide stability. Four padded side cushions support shins and arms.

"Wanna try it?"

"Sure do!" A pause. "But without the straps."

"Fine with me."

We pick up the bench and lug it outside. I point to a spot in a grove of dwarf banana trees. Kalani carries the front of the bench, and I bring up the rear, as it were. God, I'm turned on looking at his broad shoulders, traps and supple back muscles. We stop, and raucous myna birds squawk from the top of the catchment. A mongoose darts from a lava outcrop, stops, sits on its haunches, stares, blinks and retreats.

"Romantic, sort of," he says, fondling a bunch of dwarf bananas. I nod.

"Be right back." He caresses the leather and I return to the house.

A few minutes later I skip off the lanai with a bucket of towels, lube and bottled water, but catch myself and transform a jog into a saunter, pacing myself to appear relaxed, not overly eager. He's already stretched out on the bench, head sunk into the leather and pointed toward my private rain forest. I can't tell if his eyes are open or closed.

Jesus, Mary, and Joseph, I think as I stare at the luscious feast spread before me. Mom would never have approved of my language, and couldn't begin to comprehend the situation, but, hey, we do find our own way.

"Water?" I whisper.

Kalani jerks his head, a startled motion, like he had been dozing. "*Mahalo*."

We drink, him still in a prone position. "Relax. I'll take it from here."

He gulps, puts his head down, and I rub his back.

A loud clatter interrupts our reverie. He jerks up.

"What's that?" He's trembling.

"The pot police whirlybird just lollygagged by," I answer. "Nothing to worry about. Sometimes they drop a rope and rappel into a yard or field, but we're clean. No suspicious plants here. Now try to relax again."

"Jesus. Exciting neighborhood."

"Yeah. This is a hippie town. You know that."

He plops down.

I spread my rainbow towel on the lawn in a neat rectangle, kneel, spread his cheeks and stare. A gorgeous ass, a puckered hole to die for framed by a few black hairs, looks like a sloppy shave, but no, it's almost hairless like the rest of his body. Not like the *haole* forest sprouting between my buns.

I blow a steady column of air around his hole, he squirms, and then I attack with my tongue. I lick and savor his musky maleness, cover the perimeter with spit and lick it off. A late afternoon Hawaiian picnic! My curled tongue pushes as deep as possible, and I tongue-fuck him. He squirms and moans and I capture him, arms around his thighs, face buried until I surface for air. I sit back and swat his ass.

"Ohmygod!" His cry begins as a moan and crescendos to a howl of exhilaration.

Might be his first time, I think. *Or, perhaps, his best time,* I add with self-congratulatory satisfaction.

We slurp more water. He rises up on two hands and looks back at me.

"I'd like to fuck you," I announce.

"Yeah, bro, yeah, I'm all yours." He slumps into the leather and clutches the hand rests.

Better hold on, boy, here we go.

I don a rubber. I lube his asshole with one hand, and with my other hand jerk his cock, which is hidden under the bench but not difficult to find since it's hard. Very hard. Then I enter him.

Sort of slowly, but then I plunge to the limit. He gasps.

"It's okay, we're there."

He grunts.

I grab his hips and pump. There's no holding back. I flop onto his back and heave my weight into my lunges. I bite his neck.

"You're a good fuck, boy," I growl.

"Thank you, Daddy," he answers with what breath he can summon during my assault.

"Puma is fine. No role-playing. Just you and me."

"Okay, Puma."

"That's better."

I stare into the jungle, not noticing anything in particular, content to be embraced by nature. I gently slap his shoulders with both hands in time to my pelvic rhythm, and then alternate hands as I smack his ass.

Whack! Oof!

Whack! Oof!

"Like that boy?"

"Yes, Puma!"

Praise to the Hawaiian god or goddess of sex, I think. I could go on like this all day.

"I'm going to come, Puma."

"Go for it boy, I'm with you."

I feel his trembling, the precursor to his eruption, and I join him.

Kalani lifts himself onto his knees and elbows and lets out a mighty bellow. I follow a few seconds later with a loud "Aaaah!" He collapses onto the bench; I rest on his back and soften within him.

Our breathing slackens, and I pull out. He sits sideways on the bench, legs dangling over the side, palms on the leather. He looks up at the sky.

"Whew, quite a ride, a ride and a half."

"Glad you enjoyed it."

"More than enjoy. It was, it was, well—"

I put my index finger across his lips. "Shhh," I say, and lean into him and kiss him. Our long, floppy dicks rub like two mating snakes. I pull him to his feet and lead him to the patio. We sit and stare silently into the yard. Two red cardinals chase each other, swooping and diving like a World War I air battle, fighting for a lone plain-Jane female watching from a bird feeder. We chuckle in unison.

"Lots of red around here," Kalani observes.

"A great color."

"Why? What's so special about it?"

"Well, it's snazzy. Always wore red shorts when running laps at the college track after work, or on morning neighborhood runs. And, believe it or not, a recent study shows that reactions become more forceful when you see red—enhances speed, if only briefly. Like a danger signal."

I pause and put my hand on his thigh. "Or maybe an invitation."

"Hmm. Yeah. Female baboons get red bottoms when they wanna get laid, I learned in bio class."

"There's that. And your bottom has a nice blush to it."

Kalani squirms. Cute beyond measure. "Feels good, though."

We're silent for a few moments.

"I noticed that some of your whips are, what do you say, braided in red and black."

"Yes, by special order."

More silence.

"Some of them seemed, like, kinda soft."

"Like a car wash."

"Why would anyone wanna be whipped?"

"'Cause they enjoy the sensual trip."

"But some of them looked mean, real mean."

"Yes, it can be painful. In fact, I've used a signal whip—that's a short single tail whip used in dog sledding—to make a series of *x*'s across a person's back."

"Wow."

"But sometimes the person leaves their body and goes, who knows where. And, on rare occasions I go with them—the whips take care of themselves."

A long pause.

"As a top, I actually enjoy the sensual trips. It's more of a challenge to be warm and loving using a whip."

Calmness hangs between us.

"Would you flog me?" A slight hesitation. "Sir?"

"Yes." *Oh, yes, indeed.*

"Outside?"

"Where else? Stay here."

I go inside, throw a few whips over my shoulder and grab a handful of bungee cords and two soft leather wrist cuffs. Kalani stands when I approach. I put my hands on his shoulders and bore into his soul.

"You sure?"

"Uh, yes, Sir. Like, I trust you."

I put the cuffs on him, and snap the locks shut. His dick jumps with each click. I laugh.

"That's my boy. Follow me."

I grab my bucket and towel and head across the yard, boy in tow. We pass under a coconut tree and Kalani stares up at the fronds swaying in the gentle breeze.

"Coconuts were trimmed a few weeks ago," I assure him.

"Oh."

I stop at a tall, straight, very solid Ohia. I wrap the rainbow towel around the trunk, secure it with bungee cords, stuff a towel under its upper edge, and tighten another bungee seven feet up. Kalani steps up to the trunk and leans into it, his head resting on the pillow.

I tie his hands to the upper cord.

"Gotcha," I chuckle. He shudders and I blow a measured, gentle breath across his back.

"You're considerate," he says.

"I want you to be comfortable while I pummel you."

"Huh?"

"No distractions, just the whips."

"Oh."

"This is very special," I whisper.

He nods.

I rub his upper back, reveling in the firm, but supple muscles.

"Here we go," I announce.

I take my red deerskin flogger, grasp the tails near the handle, and with my other hand slide the dangling tips across his upper back, down his torso, and tease his buttcrack. He remains motionless, almost afraid to breathe.

"Relax," I command.

He inhales deeply.

"Good boy."

I take a practice swing, less to gauge distance, more so he feels the tips grazing his back. I strike his shoulder blades using a figure eight pattern, and gradually increase the intensity. He hops from one foot to the other as I progress from pats to pummels, his cries of "Ah, ah, ah," in sync with each hit. Then I strike. Hard. He screams and rears back. I wait and strike again on the other shoulder. He roars.

I throw my arms around Kalani, my torso to his back, and slither in our sweat.

"Doing okay?"

"I think so."

"Have some water." We drink.

"Ready for more?"

"I think so."

"Are you sure?"

"Yes, Sir!"

"That's what I want to hear."

I grab my black, very solid leather flogger.

I hit each shoulder blade a few times and move to his ass. And what an ass it is! I crouch a tad, steady myself and use a gentle backhand stroke on each cheek, switching from hand to hand.

"That's a big whip," he says.

"Yep." I raise my voice. "Don't worry about the tool, just sink into the sensation," I shout.

Then I lay into him, let him have it, little or no mercy, but a modicum of care.

He screams. And screams. And screams.

I back off and throw water across his ass. He jumps and yells. His backside is a uniform deep red, almost burgundy. His breathing slackens. We share more water, he gulping, me sipping.

I hoist my one-hundred-twenty-tail whip, custom made with no small amount of grumbling from the master whip maker. The twenty-six-inch-long soft tails are green, black, and turquoise, with a few red tails peeking from the center. I slide them down Kalani's back and then strike. It takes a strong arm to maneuver this instrument of pleasure. I hit his shoulders as hard as possible; the tails splay and cover his upper torso.

"Holy shit," he gasps.

"My car wash whip," I yell.

I continue pummeling him, his body slumps, his weight supported by the cuffs. A few more strokes and I stop. I touch his shoulder blades with my palms.

"We're done," I say between labored breaths. His head jerks to attention.

"Huh?"

"It's all over, you can rest now." I undo his cuffs, slide the towel to the base of the tree and guide him to rest against it.

He shakes his head. "Where was I, Sir?"

"Only you know that, boy."

I kiss him and lead him into the bedroom. I move my stack of books and notes from the king size bed. I spoon him, my arms wrapped around my prize. Eventually we stretch out and doze. An hour or so later I climb out of bed and raise the blinds. He rolls over. I point at a palm tree, seventy or so feet tall, ivy swirling about its variegated trunk, climbing and reaching for the newborn coconuts just under its spreading fronds. Nature's stately umbrella gleams in the low sun, framed by white, downy clouds wandering through an azure sky streaked with pink. I climb back in bed.

"Beautiful," he says. "Thanks."

He puts his arm around my shoulder.

"Lots of books around here."

"Yep."

"Lots of subjects."

"Yep," I respond, running my hand along his chest, trying not to grab his hard dick. "What's your major?"

"Astronomy."

"Continue, please, I'm interested. Very much so."

"Hmm," he replies. "Unusual. Most folks don't give a damn."

I smile. "I'm waiting," I coax and nibble his nipple, teasing my teeth into a bite.

"As a boy," he begins, "I was intrigued at the glistening white domes on top of Mona Kea."

"Observatories," I interject.

"Yeah, sponsored by several countries. I visited, and was hooked. What do you do...I mean, did, like...like before you retired?" He leans over, tugs a few of my chest hairs, and pinches my nipple.

"I was an optical engineer, specialized in optical coatings."

"Like, holy shit!"

"I've supervised the coating of more than one large telescope mirror. And designed the coatings."

"They could use you up there."

"Well, those days are gone. Besides, it's too damn cold at fifteen-thousand feet. I left the snow behind me when I moved from the mainland." I shiver and pause. "I also fabricated minute mirrors, like for endoscopes."

He roars, spits on his finger and goes for my asshole.

I sink into the pillows and close my eyes. Silence. I look up and he's untangling one of the flat, red cargo straps dangling from the bedpost. He ties my wrists together with an evil grin. I smile and nod. He wraps the remainder of the cord around my ankles, pulls them to my wrists and hog-ties me on my back. He cinches the slack to the iron cross frame above my head and shoves a pillow under my butt. My hole is exposed, open, puckered, whatever. I'm a pretzel, not bad for my age, and almost embarrassed.

"Nice *haole* hairy hole," he states matter-of-factly. He grabs a condom from the bedside table and lubes his dick and a few fingers. I again close my eyes.

A finger probes and enters, then two, then three. He chuckles.

"Could probably stick my whole hand up here."

"It's been done. Up to the elbow."

"Jesus, Mary and Joseph! So I don't have to be gentle."

"Well..."

He plunges in, and I swallow his fat dick. My cock rubs against his smooth chest. He's fucking me, and I'm fucking the cleft between his pecs.

"Never done this before," he gasps.

"Could've fooled me. Where're you learn the rope trick?"

"Watched a few flicks. Now shut up, and screw, Puma!"

"Yes, Sir, boy!"

I have no choice, I can't move. I revel in his having his way with me. Our eyes meet. Mine glisten over. *Yeah, its good, it's very, very good,* I think. I tremble, almost shake, in my secure bondage. He smiles.

"Glad I can give you a good time, Puma. You deserve it, like, like...lots."

Kalani wraps his arms around me, we can't get any closer, can't couple any tighter. We're one sweaty ball. He wiggles and moans. He pauses, perhaps to savor the moment, his anticipation, his awe.

"Jesus, Puma, I love you," he whispers. He comes in me—I feel his gentle shudders. But he doesn't pull out. He massages my cock, and I groan and cover his throat with cum. He leans back.

"*Mahalo* for giving me this," he says.

Who's giving who what? I think.

"Thank you," I manage to utter as he wipes off his neck.

Kalani unties me and we rest side by side, our inner hands clasped together. He looks over at me.

"You have a nice tan," he says.

"Probably because I have a little Cherokee in me. Dad was from Georgia."

"Holy shit! That sorta makes us, like, well, related?"

"Well, hardly."

His kiss is slow but vigorous. Almost sucks the breath out of me.

"Will I see you again?" I ask.

"Oh, yes," he answers. "Soon, very soon." He pauses. "I'd like to give you a Hawaiian friendship bracelet."

I sit up. "I'm honored, deeply honored. That's, that's very special."

"Yeah, very. I'll bring it over my next visit. Gotta get home now."

Where? I wonder. *And to whom*? Well, no matter.

Kalani sits up and looks over his shoulder as he traipses to the living room. I follow. He gets dressed and I hold the door open. I trail him to his truck.

He punches me in the chest with his fist.

"Aloha, bro," he says.

"Aloha," I respond.

He hops in the cab. I watch my Hawaiian boy drive away, his left hand waving through the open window. I'm standing at the end of the walkway, naked, half hard. Jesus, what the hell would the Fed Ex driver think of this outfit?

In truth, I don't care. I like showing off and look who it brought me today.

I stroll into the house.

CHISHOLM TRAIL BOYS

Dale Chase

We crossed three rivers on the Chisholm Trail while driving two thousand head of cattle from San Antonio to Abilene. Each time we got the herd across and settled, I allowed the men to bathe. At the Brazos River, two weeks out, we lay over a few days to rest both ourselves and the cattle as we had driven hard to tire them so they'd be more manageable. We also used this time to brand calves born along the way.

The men bathed in shifts as some were required to watch the herd and see to branding, thus five or six stripped naked and waded in. As trail boss, I was free to enjoy looking on, which I never failed to do as young cowboys are a pleasing sight.

I kept myself in the saddle since it would not do for the boss to splash about with his men, not to mention the embarrassment at having his dick stiff while among them. I always bathed later on, alone, and as I was heated up by then, I always pulled my dick and enjoyed a good come.

This trip was my eighth as trail boss and I had lost count

of how many drives I'd ridden before that, not only on the Chisholm but the Western and Goodnight trails. I knew the territory well and enjoyed life in the open. As I was in charge of the whole operation, I decided every stop we made and spent much time scouting ahead for good grass and water. My second man had some authority and kept things going while I was absent. This fellow was Wiley Robbins, until he was thrown and broke his leg in so many places he quit and went to live with a sister in Illinois. A new second was with me now, Duane Shafter, a fine-looking fellow who, at thirty, was four years my junior. A skilled horseman, he was also good at settling disputes and teaching the new men our way of life. At the Brazos he rode up alongside me as I sat on my horse watching the men bathe. "A fine sight," he said.

I had never spoken of my enjoyment at watching but Duane seemed a good sort so I agreed. "That it is."

"Look at Lovell," Duane countered. "I think he's doing himself."

Lovell, a striking Texan no more than eighteen, had a familiar arch to him and the water churned at his front, no doubt due to a hand active below the surface. I noted the fixed jaw of a man having a come and this stirred me to no end.

"If we were closer," Duane noted, "I bet we could see spunk on the water."

I looked at him then and he smiled most wickedly and rode off. This captured my attention but not enough to keep me from the men, who had little concern at the boss looking on.

Some washed themselves while others lazed about. A few got to splashing one another and I always liked this as it usually led to a tussle, which had a good chance of getting stiff cocks into view. Occasionally, a fellow would float on his back, dick up like a pole, and I would suffer such intense arousal I'd shift in the saddle to accommodate my hard cock.

This was our first full day at the Brazos River and, as it was late morning, the men in the water were the first shift. My vantage point was well up from the shore but I could see it all. When Lovell moved to the shallow, ready to get out, I became most attentive, knowing what he'd done to himself. The sight of his spent cock added to my pleasurable unrest. That he tugged it most absently as he stretched to the sun caused my mouth to dry out to such extent I sought my canteen. He stood dripping, allowing nature to dry him while calling out to the others, all laughing and cutting up. Then Neal Beck swam to the shallow and stood, his cock hard, and I wondered what he would do with it. I leaned forward as he began to work his dick without caring who saw. The other men ignored him, save for Lowell who, still drying, looked over to watch. Soon Beck was spewing come and I became so aroused I rode off to a secluded spot up river, got down off my horse, opened my pants to free my throbbing cock and took about three pulls before letting go a gusher.

I got back to camp in time for the cook to call out dinner and I ate sitting next to my second, speaking of our work until he turned the subject elsewhere. "Fine bunch of men," he said. "Hard workers to a one. Striking bunch, too. Fine specimens of manhood."

I did not know his purpose in such talk as my former second had never spoken this way. "Beck is especially fine bodied," Duane went on. "Don't you think?"

Here I felt somewhat ashamed, as I had feasted on Beck's pulling his dick. "Yes," I managed. "He is strong."

"Well, that too."

I finished my meal and rode out to look at the herd, which was well settled and munching grass. I spoke to a couple of the men on duty, reminding them they'd be relieved shortly to get their dinner and have a bath.

"Sounds good, Boss," said Johnny Roop, a youngster of nineteen on his first drive. He rode drag behind the herd and ate more dust than the rest of us, thus I knew he'd appreciate washing it off. All cowboys started at the back and all discovered how much trail dirt can accumulate on a man. Laying over was a treat for these fellows and Roop was most happy at present. He was dark haired but fair skinned, looking untried in every aspect of life. I wanted very much to see him in the water, as a young dick is hard more than not.

When the shift had changed. I held myself back awhile as I did not want to appear eager. And holding back made it better as I thought on the naked men, Roop especially, washing himself, playing with a fresh pink cock. Finally I got back into the saddle and rode down to the river.

Six were in the water and two were up close to each other. One was Johnny Roop, whose gaze was fixed on Wes Flynn who was three years his senior. I knew Flynn as this was his fourth year with the outfit. He had a thick body, a big dick and was known to fuck anything that moved. As he spoke to Roop, the boy smiled. The two then moved to deeper water and I watched as Flynn got behind Roop, wrapped his arms around the boy and pulled him close. From their movements I knew they were fucking.

Roop wore a blissful expression as he took the big cock. Then one hand dropped down and I could see it working his own prick and churning the water. It took but a couple minutes for them to do it and I thought I would come in my pants at the sight. I did not notice my second riding up until the pair had parted. "Some fuck," he said.

I wanted to agree but could not find words as it occurred to me only then that my new second had designs on me. I knew myself receptive but, much as I'd left come all up and down the Chisholm Trail, I had never fucked my second. Nor any of the hired men. I always cut loose at trail's end in Abilene and there were some men back in Texas I did regular but on the trail I relieved my need by hand, what with being trail boss. It would not be good for the men to catch me fucking as this placed a man in vulnerable circumstances, I don't care how big or how hard his dick. Now here was Duane making an advance when he knew me aroused at sight of the men.

"You like to watch," I said to avoid what had become plain.

"No better sight than naked boys with hard dicks," he said. "Best part of driving cattle."

"I like to look," I confessed.

"That all?"

"It wouldn't do for the boss to get up to things."

"Even if the men don't know?"

Here I turned to him. "What are you up to?"

"Ride with me," he said and he pulled his horse away and started up river. I looked back at the men lazing in the water. And I followed Duane.

He rode a short distance to a where a trail let to a rocky outcropping overlooking the water. On top was a roomy bluff of smooth stone. Duane hopped off his horse and tied it to a nearby tree, then squatted down to look upon the river. I watched him only a second before doing the same.

The men were a little ways off but the view remained good. I squatted beside Duane and together we looked on, the men now splashing one another, all of them at play. "I'd venture they'll do more without you down there looking on," Duane said.

"You think?"

"Well, looka that. Parsons keeps diving under at Zeder's

front. I'll venture he's sucking dick for as long as his breath holds out. Look how Zeder is pounding the water. Parsons is going to bring him off."

Parsons then popped up and after some manipulation, began to hump his friend front to front. "Rubbing dicks," Duane said. "Holy shit, I cannot stand it." Here he stood and undid his pants, pushed them down along with his under drawers. His cock was stiff. "I'll bend if you'll do me," he said. "Otherwise I'll use my hand, but what's the point of that as don't tell me you're not ready."

I looked down at the humping men, then at Duane standing with his pants down and his dick out. And I did not have to weigh the situation. I bared my own necessities, turned and bent him, then shoved my prick up his butthole. As I had not had a proper fuck since we left Texas, I was most agitated at getting into another man and I rode him hard and quick to attain a powerful come. His knees nearly buckled as I emptied and I had to grab him at the waist to keep him from collapsing, but we managed and I spurted every drop I had into his passage. When I was done, I pulled out and stood breathless while he turned to me, prick still up. "Suck me," he said and though I was still taking in breath to regain myself, I dropped to my knees and got my mouth onto him. He was ready to blow and I had but seconds of licking and pulling before he shot his stuff into my throat. I fed most eagerly as I liked to swallow a man's cream and I kept on sucking until he went soft. Only then did I release him.

Soon as we parted, he looked down at the men. "All quiet now," he said, "but still a sight."

"Look at Parsons and Zeder lying on the bank," I replied. "You know they'll want to get at it again. If they go back into the water, it will be to fuck."

We continued such conversation awhile, then lay down on the smooth rock so we could be comfortable together and keep looking. We did not pull up our pants and I got a hand on Duane's dick, tugging as I lay behind him, my own cock parked at his rear. I knew we would need another go if we kept the current view.

A good hour had to have passed with no more action below than men rolling about in the water. Some even took time to wash themselves and we decided this was appealing as the men ran their hands over themselves at length. "They spend more time washing their dicks than anything," Duane noted.

"Except their cracks," I replied.

One fellow, I think it was Ames, had his legs spread and was washing just that place, running his fingers up and down until, I swear, he started to fuck himself. "Look, he's got a finger in," I said.

"Wishful thinking, Bud. He's just washing."

"The inside? Look closer. He's spending way too much time in his butthole."

"Maybe it's full of spunk," Duane ventured.

"Maybe it needs to be."

We kept on like this, our talk downright filthy, which got me stiff again. "Ease back," I told him and as he pushed against me I got my prick up him. We then lay watching the men and fucking at the same time and I shot another load while he worked his cock to spew onto the rock. After this, I said we had best get back. "Not good for first and second to be absent too long."

Back in camp we separated and kept well apart the rest of the day. The last shift of bathers hit the water after supper as it was a warm night. Dusk was already upon us but there was still enough light for me to get a good look as I especially wanted to see Dobson, who stood well over six feet and carried a bulge in his pants. Sure enough, he stripped to reveal a horse cock and I could not tell if it had a natural girth or was starting to get hard. Either way, I was most impressed and wished Duane was beside me so we could comment.

Much as I thought about making up a double bedroll with Duane, as men sometimes did, I made myself act like we had not gotten up to anything. As I lay under the stars, I could not help but handle my dick as I recalled both the sight of the naked men and the feel of fucking my second. I had a good idea he was occupied much the same.

"How long we gonna lay over?" the cook asked me when a week had passed at the Brazos. Though many of the men chose not to bathe every day, enough did to make watching a pleasure. Duane and I did so to excess, both while on our horses at the river and also while fucking like rabbits atop that bluff. In such circumstance, I did not want to move on yet knew we had lost enough time. The calves were branded, the cattle docile, and a long road lay ahead. "Tomorrow," I told the cook.

He studied me which I did not especially like as cooks tend to be good judges of men. On the other hand, if he found out I'd been at Duane, he would hold the confidence. Still, I did not want my dick business known to anyone but the man I was putting it to.

Since I'd trapped myself into breaking camp next day, I told Duane the decision, then rode ahead to scout our next stop. I sent Duane to a farm I knew to trade a calf for whatever vegetables and fruit the farmer might spare. This was common practice on the trail and, as we had a surplus of calves, it helped the farmer as much as us. As I did my scouting while already knowing the next likely stop, I thought about the men back in the water, picturing them all standing in a row pulling their dicks for me while I fucked Duane on the shore. This got me so worked up that when I stopped at a creek to water my horse, I got out my prick and pulled it to release. I then went on to the planned location and, finding it agreeable, rode back to camp.

That afternoon I rode down to the river to see what was about and found four men circled in shallow water, all working their pricks as if in competition. Backs were arched, legs were spread, and it was a sight to behold. And there was Duane on his horse, watching the show.

"Look at them, seeing who can shoot the most."

"Like to be in that circle with my mouth open," I ventured. Just then three other men came down to the shore and shucked their clothes. "Let's go up to the bluff," I suggested. "I need to get at you."

"Suits me fine since this is likely our last."

"Until I find us a spot on the Cimarron."

This was our next river to cross and therefore the next place for the men to wash. It would take several days to get there so I wanted to get at Duane good and long. He turned his horse and started up river and I followed, my prick already getting hard.

We got our pants and under drawers off entirely as had become our practice. I took him standing the first time, both of us looking down upon the men. "Not much going on," he said as I pumped in and out of him.

"Plenty up here," I noted just before I came.

I turned my face to the sun as I emptied into him, catching not only the sun's rays but some of nature's sweet air. I felt I had gone to heaven by way of Duane Shafter's bottom.

Once done, I pulled out and we sat awhile. The men were quiet below, bathing or lazing. "You know they all need a fuck," Duane offered.

"Looks like you'll have to go down there and do it," I replied.

"Tempting."

Just then Reed Wooley and Kurt Lovell began to splash one another. "Look, they're starting up," I said.

The two romped some, churned up the water, then quieted. "Lovell is pulling Wooley's dick," Duane said.

"That he is. And Wooley has hold of Lovell. Can't keep their hands off a dick, be it their own or a friend's."

At this Duane reached for mine and I got a hand onto his and we sat playing with each other awhile before I was stiff again. I then put him onto all fours, turned so he could still see down below, and managed a good long fuck.

By the time we reached the Cimarron River, the cattle were unruly from hot weather and lack of water. Two of the usual watering holes along the way had dried to mud, which was a disappointment. A steer can go a couple days without water but they become a danger because soon as they smell it ahead, they run for it. Many a herd has stampeded for no reason but a shift in the wind.

I made sure the men were sharp and in full force as we neared the Cimarron, extras on point and alongside. Didn't matter. Twenty-five men and two thousand head of thirsty cattle are no match. I was up front when they broke and no matter our efforts, they went all directions until we had nothing resembling a herd. The only good part of this kind of break is they all ran into the water. The bad part was they lacked room and thus some trampled their brethren while others ran up river and down river, getting into rougher places where the current swept them against rocks and drowned some. We reached the river at nine in the morning and did not get the herd to the opposite shore until dusk. There was no stop for dinner and no thought to personal needs. Every man made every effort to get the cattle across, even when they would not budge.

We were all soaked by the time we had a herd again. While the men quieted the cattle, Duane and I rode up and down river to count the number lost which came to twenty-six. There were always losses on a cattle drive. Twenty-six was not bad.

The cook was the only man not chasing steers so he made us a fine supper, even as he complained at having no help to dig his fire pit and bring him wood. "I don't want to hear it," I told him, "else next time you'll be out there with us." That settled him down considerably.

Ma Nature was at least kindly toward us in leaving the night warm so we could remove our wet clothes and set them out to dry. Those with spare shirts could change but most, me included, had but one pair of pants. Stripping these off, we remained in under drawers, which gradually dried. We were a sorry-looking bunch, most in drawers that had seen too many days.

Duane and I had now made it a habit to lay our bedrolls alongside each other and away from the men. While they slept on one side of the chuck wagon, we sought the other and none dared to question the arrangement. When night fell this particular time, there was no campfire and no socializing. Everyone was too tired to care. By the time the cattle lay down to sleep the men had long been snoring.

As we had no visual entertainments, Duane and I had taken to pulling each other's dicks in the dark of night. Nearly a month into the drive, we had become much attached. Now we lay working each other.

Duane's breathing soon began to pick up and he started bucking, then muffled a squeal as he let go his load. He stopped pulling me as he did so, then once he'd quieted he got back to it. When he had me near the peak, he suddenly threw off my blanket, crawled over and took me into his mouth. I held back a cry as his tongue and lips worked my prick to a frenzy. I then began to spurt and he took it all, swallowing as if he could not get enough. When I had finished, he gave my cockhead a last lick, then lay back down.

"Christ, Duane, what was that?"

"If you don't know..." he chuckled.

"I mean what are you up to? The men might see."

"See what? The moon is a sliver. We're no more than shadow and besides, they are all asleep."

"Still, if someone woke and happened to look our way he could see. A head bobbing on a dick is noticeable even in shadow."

"Well then, I am sorry I sucked your prick," he replied in a huff.

"I don't mean it that way so stop carrying on. I just don't want the men seeing us get up to it."

He said nothing more and I held off pointing out he was pouting like a baby. Next morning he was up and gone before I opened my eyes. "We gonna lay over?" he asked when I rode out and found him and several others pulling dead cattle from the river. We wouldn't take time to bury them but at least we could prevent them fouling the water.

"No, not with dead animals around," I told him. "We can lay over at the Red River."

"That's a good ten days."

"Yes, it is," I said. I then rode off to scout our next location, which I would have done the day before had things not gotten out of hand. Fortunately, a spring up ahead was down but not out, leaving enough to water us all but not much more. Didn't much matter as nobody seemed to want to get wet. The spot had sparse grass in a split between low hills but not a tree in sight. Camp was made, the cattle now quiet, and Duane and I again pulled dicks under the stars.

When I rode ahead to scout the next day's noon stop, he asked to come along. We rode at a good clip until we reached Copper Springs where the water was gone.

"Need rain," he offered as we looked down at dried mud.

"Well, thank you for the enlightenment."

"Nobody saw," he then said, going back to a closed subject. "If they had seen there would be talk."

"How do you know there isn't?"

"I keep an eye out."

"It was a foolish move."

"You didn't exactly put me off," he noted.

"Well, Christ, no I did not. A man ready to come is not rational and you were counting on that. Next thing you'll want me to fuck you right there in camp."

"Not there but how about here?" he said.

"You are shitting me."

He hopped off his horse. "Right here, between the horses, do it standing. You know you need it much as me." Here he undid his pants and pushed them down. His dick sprang up and he grabbed it. "Get down here and fuck me, Bud. Else I'll be pestering to suck you in the night."

I looked around. Though in the open, I saw not man nor beast nor even bird. And Christ, I did want to do him.

We stood between the horses, him with his hands on his saddle, legs spread, me going at him with a fury. The horses snickered and snorted, their own cocks likely hard at the smell of sex. I did not take long as I was pent up and when I let go I raised a cry, such was the release. Duane had a hand on his dick and seconds after I'd spurted he did likewise, calling out he was coming, swearing some, then lost to the spew.

When we had emptied I wrapped my arms around him and nuzzled his neck. "Fixes everything," I said.

"For now."

"You are a greedy man, Duane Shafter."

He reached back and tugged my dick. "I sure as hell am."

We rode on some miles but found no good water and sparse grass so I finally called it and we galloped back to camp. Supper was over but the cook had saved us steaks, biscuits and gravy, which we wolfed down. That night Duane did not suck my cock.

We were fortunate to find water the day before we hit the Red River, thus the cattle did not break and run as before. They crossed the river most orderly, which cheered the men to such extent they sang around the campfire after supper.

"We'll lay over a couple days," I told them, which got hoots from all. "Almost halfway now and you boys have done good work so you can have a rest."

The Red River was my favorite as it ran into little eddies that were ideal to laze in. Those wanting brisk water had only to move down stream to find rocks that set the current churning. Trees lined the shore, offering welcome shade, but there was no bluff on which to play around with Duane.

As before, the men bathed in shifts and as before, I rode down to watch. The urge was well upon me when Duane rode up and said to follow him.

"There's no place around here," I told him.

"There is up river."

I had my eyes on Lovell and Beck who were in an eddy having a fuck. "Just a minute," I said, nodding their way.

"Beautiful sight," Duane observed as we shared the spectacle.

"You are right in that I do need more than looking," I admitted when the men finished.

We got away maybe a quarter mile up river. Here it quieted alongside a sandy shore, trees curtaining it from sight.

"You can't see the men from here," I said.

"That all you want?"

Duane was off his horse and stripping naked before I could reply. "Get down here and let's do it in the water," he said. "Nobody is up this way."

I looked around. He was right. He seemed to have a natural ability to scout places to fuck. "Undress," he coaxed as he slipped into the water. He paddled out and lay floating on his back, dick up, and I could not resist. I undressed and waded in, then swam out to grab his cock, which made him playful. We splashed and grappled until I could stand it no longer. I pushed him to the shallow, which was maybe a foot deep, got him onto all fours and shoved in.

As I rode him I decided we could laze the afternoon here and fuck to excess because one was not going to be enough. And I wanted to suck his dick, maybe while he sucked mine, and maybe even get my tongue up his crack. The need to wallow was upon me.

My juice boiled at such thoughts and I started to pound his bottom just as a commotion stirred nearby. As my stuff began the rise a calf burst through the trees and into the water not twenty feet away and behind it two of my men in pursuit. Their horses splashed into the water, then stopped, but I kept on pumping, not giving a damn at being seen as I needed to come. Shooting my stuff into Duane, I kept on until satisfied, even as the riders stopped to look.

It was Wayne Zeder and Johnny Roop doing their job rounding up strays, and as I pulled out of Duane I had no idea what to do. I stood up and found Roop looking down at my prick, much as I had looked at his. When he began to grin, I saw we had a fair exchange of places, him gazing upon my privates instead of the other way around, and so I allowed him all he wanted. I even reached down to tug my dick, which made him yank his reins, his horse snorting at the intrusion. Duane, meanwhile, was on his feet and looking from the men to me and back.

It crossed my mind, since we had been seen in the worst way, that we might throw caution to the wind and invite the boys in for who knows what. As I looked at Roop who still feasted on my naked body, it sounded a good idea but before I could speak, Zeder said to Roop, "C'mon, we should get back. Leave the boss to his business."

When they'd roped the calf and ridden off, I had to laugh. I grabbed Duane and pulled him into the water. "What's so damned funny?" he asked as I got him into my arms.

"Only fair they get a look," I said. "I've been watching boys for eight years. Guess it's their turn."

"You were on drives before that," Duane noted. "Bet you did a lot of looking early on."

I thought back to my first drive at eighteen when I was wide eyed and ripe. My knowledge of men began on that trip, putting it to another drag rider while on night guard. We did it standing between the horses, both of us covered in trail dust. This recall now played before me like some dirty show and I was grateful for the view. It had not occurred to me to look back since my job was always looking ahead and I found I had missed something in failing to consider myself. I had a well-muscled body and good prick which Duane now began to tug. I got my hands onto his bottom and as I slipped into his crack, I let my younger self play along. I kept the image running as my finger pushed into Duane's hole and I wondered what all we would see next.

NAKED SUMMER BLUES

Ron Radle

They were an odd couple physically—but in a good way.

Tyler Patrick stood just over six feet and had short brown hair, a goatee and the build of a college heavyweight wrestler. He was obviously and openly handsome, the most conspicuous features of his face being his large brown eyes and wide, smiling mouth with thick lips. His partner, Cole O'Neal, presented an opposing portrait in good looks: he was five eight with thick blond hair that he wore past his ears; startling, steel-blue eyes and a mouth as wide as Tyler's but more comical than sensuous—although its sensuous possibilities were ample enough. His features were offset by a frankly large nose that curved down from the edge of his forehead and drew to a thick point over his mouth. It would be an attractive feature as long as he was young; when he got older it might prove, like his mouth, more comic. He was almost as solidly built as Tyler, and actually better defined, his torso a hairless structure of smooth muscle. I would say that neither of them could have been more than twenty.

I learned their names in the short time it took us to become friendly. We were neighbors of a sort. We shared adjoining rooms at the Tropic Isles motel in Myrtle Beach, South Carolina, a place valued more for its convenient distance to the beach than for any other amenities. I had been coming down to Myrtle Beach and staying at Tropic Isles for a few years by then. Alone but not always alone. The first few times, I vacationed with my lover, who was more of a mountain man than a beachcomber and never cared for the sunny sandiness of the beach. When we broke up, I continued the tradition alone, but I enjoyed the freedom.

My introduction to Tyler and Cole came wordlessly. I had seen them go in and out of their room and heard them padding around. They had nodded a curt hello to me, which I returned. Then late the night of their arrival, I was awakened to the sound of a regular knocking against the wall that divided our rooms, and of men's voices in conflict, or what sounded like conflict. After clearing my head, I realized they were not fighting, but fucking. Their voices took on all the old familiar commands of heated lovemaking—*Don't stop! More, more! Yeah, that way! Oh, baby yes! Fuck me harder*!—punctuated by each shouting out the other's name. That was the end of sleep for me. I spent the rest of the night listening to them cavort through the wall for hours. *Oh, youth*! At twenty-eight I wasn't sure if I could keep it up as long as they were. I took advantage of the situation, though, by taking my own cock in hand and stroking it to the rhythm of their rutting. And, hours later, even after I could barely eke out a last, pathetic dribble of cum, they were still going strong.

The next morning we happened to be leaving our rooms at the same time. They were dressed in flowery shirts and shorts and flip-flops, as was I. We smiled awkwardly at each other.

Then I went ahead and said what was on all our minds: "After last night, I would think you boys would be too exhausted to leave the room."

They eyed each other and laughed.

"Were we too loud?" Tyler asked sheepishly.

"Sorry," Cole offered.

"No, no, it's all right. I enjoyed it *almost* as much y'all did." They eyed each other again with guilty grins. "In fact I'm surprised *I* can leave the room. Y'all put on a hell of a show. Felt like I was right there with you."

"Sorry," Cole said again. His magnificent blue eyes were a reflection of the ocean just below us.

"We'll make it up to you," Tyler added ambiguously, and my knees went weak.

That's when I found out their names and that they came from the same part of South Carolina as I did, the northwestern upcountry. They were celebrating the end of their first year in college with this beach trip. When they were done telling, they looked at me out of curiosity. It was my turn to spill the beans about myself. I told them I was general manager for a well-known chain bookstore in one of the biggest cities in the state. The boys' aptitude for academia became clear when they wrinkled their noses at hearing where I worked.

"Don't worry," I assured them quickly. "I don't have to read the books. I just have to sell them."

They seemed relieved, but I was disappointed. No matter how far and wide I looked, I probably never would find their elusive combination of brains *and* brawn.

We parted ways after an awkward pause, but I didn't completely lose sight of them. They parked their towels and drink cooler not too far from me. This proximity gave me the chance to study them without being too obvious. They shed their shirts after a while, and right away I felt a stirring in my crotch at the sight of their young muscles. After a while the hot summer sun and my own lack of sleep conspired to make me drift off into a pleasant reverie...

Tyler and Cole were crouched on their knees on either side of me in the sand, buck naked, feeding their considerable hard, young dicks into my starving mouth. I alternated from one cock to the other, back and forth, licking and sucking wildly, my hands occupied with each set of balls, squeezing them to a point that should have hurt them but, in my fantasy, didn't. Meanwhile they reached down with one hand each to jerk me off together and to return the same abuse to my balls, and it wasn't long before the three of us were quivering, electrified flesh, the sperm-spark igniting in our nuts and zapping to the stem of our pricks. The boys groaned first and fired their thick loads onto my face and chest and into my hair. Then I let loose, and my cum spurted like a geyser. They dropped on top of me, and we mixed fluids while kissing and laughing...

"Hey there," someone said. I awoke from my nap to find the real Tyler and Cole staring down at me. They were completely dressed and looked more concerned than horny. "You best turn over," Tyler said, "or you'll be red as a beet. You've been lying there a good while now."

I looked at my blistering skin and turned over immediately. I lifted my sunglasses onto my forehead and said, "Thanks." They smiled and walked off.

Near suppertime, I was napping again in my room, this time my dreams not plagued by sex, when a knock at the door startled me awake. I wiped as much as the grog as I could from my eyes and opened it. Tyler stood in the doorway, shirtless, like the "after" picture of a muscle-building supplement advertisement. He grinned widely. He should be majoring in business, because he would have made a hell of salesman with that killer smile.

"Can I come in?" he asked.

I said nothing but stepped out of his way. He wore flower-colored jams that rested low on his hips and showed lovely cuts sloping from either side of his abdomen, pointing the way to his pubis; a hint of hair peeked out of the top of his pants. The drawstring to the drawers hung loosely. It was all I could do to keep from reaching over and jerking it to reveal Tyler in all his glory. His nipples were pink and thick and needed a good lashing of my tongue. I sat in one of the room's upholstered chairs near the door and invited Tyler to do the same. But he remained standing, staring down at me with a gleam in his eye that flashed one message: *sex*. He had come, I just knew it, to make up for the disturbance of the night before. My throat went dry at the possibility; my dick stiffened. It took great restraint not to lick lasciviously.

"I wonder if you could do me and Cole a favor," he asked finally, still smiling like a politician.

"Of course," I said right away and nearly blacked out. Would Cole be part of our amends-making screw? That would be too much!

He inched closer. I could smell his testosterone. He put his hand on my right shoulder and stroked it slowly. Then he spoke again.

"Me and Cole have always had this fantasy..." He paused to lick *his* lips in a lascivious way.

"Yes," I said, my voice barely a whisper. I just knew he was about to confess his and Cole's attraction to the idea of doing it with an older man.

"...of having somebody watch us while we fuck."

There was a slight deflation in my groin, not a total meltdown, but some softening.

"And we were wondering if you'd be the one to watch us. I mean, you seem to like us and all, and to get off on the way we look." A pause hung in the air. Tyler popped it. "So, what do you say, man?" He squeezed my shoulder with one of his strong hands. I didn't know if it was further invitation or a threat.

"Of course," I whispered, knowing I would have to apologize to my cock later.

But it was, after all, the next best thing to having sex with them, and I had gotten off, again and again, merely *listening* to them gambol the night before. This little session would have a visual component to it. They would be *naked*! Before my very eyes! And who knew? Maybe the proceedings would get so wonderfully out of hand that they would invite me to join them and make the whole thing a genuine threesome.

Tyler slipped me his card key. He and Cole would be out for a while. I could go in and station myself in the mirrored closet that held the ironing board and extra blankets and pillows. So that's what I did, leaving one of the closet doors cracked just enough for good visibility. But it was hot as hell in there, so I took off everything, and waited, naked as the day I was born.

Not long after, Tyler and Cole arrived, closing the motel room door softly behind them. Without a word, they fell into each other's arms and began groping. They had obviously fired each other up pretty good before returning to their room. They kissed deeply, as though they hadn't seen each other in days. They clawed each other's clothes off until they were as nude as I was.

Cole sighed at the sight of his lover's buff body and demanded: "Show me some guns, man!" Tyler obeyed, lifting up both his arms and flexing, his brawny biceps swelling. Cole licked his lips, then pounded the 'ceps with his fists before squeezing them with both his hands to test how hard they were. They passed.

Then Cole bent and licked Tyler's protuberant tits, flicking his tongue before digging deeply with his lips and teeth. Tyler sighed and closed his eyes. His long, fat cock rose to attention and stood between him and Cole with a slight quiver. Meanwhile, Cole's hands slid down Tyler's muscled torso till they met each other at the base of Tyler's stiff dick. Cole dropped to his knees and took it into his mouth as Tyler moaned, rolling his eyes to the ceiling. I could no longer see his big cock, but reveled in the sight of Cole's broad, bronzed back, his milk-white ass defined by his tan lines, and the contrast between his sun-tinged legs and his sandy-white soles. The boys were putting on a grand show for me, exciting the voyeur within I never knew existed. I had worked myself up to a full erection and was pounding with my right hand while my left toyed with my right nipple.

All of a sudden Tyler swooped Cole off the ground and lifted him into the air as though he weighed nothing. They looked into each other's faces and laughed. Cole bound his long legs around Tyler's hips and they joined together in a kiss. The sight of Cole's cock mashed against Tyler's chest only increased my ardor. It was as long as Tyler's but not quite as thick.

Tyler dumped Cole onto the bed, lay down beside him and took Cole's dick into his mouth, sucking like a professional all the way to the base without once gagging. At the same time, he worked first his left index finger into Cole's asshole, screwing it around and around before inserting a second finger, and then a third, finger-fucking the hole with mesmerizing vigor. He dropped to his knees, pulled out his fingers and replaced them with his face, making a feast of the asshole, fucking it with his tongue until Cole whipped around on the bed in a frenzy before finally calling out, "Fuck your tongue, dude! I want your dick!" And from my vantage point, oh, how I did, too.

Tyler was happy to oblige. He stood, spreading Cole's legs,

and managed, with no hands, to press his dickhead against his lover's asshole. With one rigorous shove he was in and pumping, resting Cole's feet against his chest and fucking with a regular rhythm that grew faster and more intense. This was hammering, not mere screwing, and I couldn't take my eyes off their bodies, pumping my cock in sync with Tyler's fuck-strokes. Tyler pounded so hard he pushed Cole a couple of inches up the bed and had to yank him back down. "Fuck this!" Cole cried in a voice shivering with pleasure. "Let's do it doggy-style!"

They rearranged themselves on the bed so that Cole presented his white butt for Tyler's edification—and in the process provided me with an even better view. This time, Tyler spread Cole's cheeks, slipping his dick in slowly before revving up with a force that quickly had Cole yelping like a dog. Tyler sped up. He threw back his head. His lips trembled, and so did I when I saw him pull his dick from Cole's hole and, crying out his lover's name, frost his back with spurt after spurt of semen. He shook as the orgasm passed through him, then gripped Cole's shoulder and turned him over to take Cole's dick into his hand and jack it. Cole's face contorted with ecstasy as Tyler pumped him; so, I'm sure, did mine, as I pumped away in the closet, sweaty and shivering with erotic excitement. Cole beat me to the punch. He bucked his hips as he spewed cum everywhere: on the bed, the floor, on Tyler. They collapsed into each other's arms.

Meanwhile my dickhead tingled. All signals were go from down below to launch. Up, up, up came the jism, and I was holding tight to my dick to keep it from flying right out of my hand. "Oh, you fuckers! You beautiful fuckers!" I yelled out as I painted the closet interior with my cum.

All of a sudden, just as I was cooling off, the mirrored door slid open. There stood Tyler, still naked.

"Aha!" he said in mock dramatic fashion. "We've got an

intruder here! A voyeur! Cole, you know the punishment for Peeping Toms, don't you?"

"I sure do," answered Cole from the bed. "A good hot double fuck from a couple of young studs."

And Tyler yanked me from the closet.

FOR REAL

Dominic Santi

"No script?"

"Do whatever you want, Zak—whatever a couple of famous porn stars do together that everybody else only dreams about."

"That's not real specific." I drank the last of my soda and sighed, loudly. Marco was a good director. I liked working with him. But his brainstorms weren't always easy to understand when he was frustrated. At the moment, we were taking a break from filming a standard fuck flick. Marco was pacing a hole in the carpet, thwapping his clipboard against his thigh and complaining about his inability to cast The Right Couple for his next creative masterpiece. I was letting my dick rest and trying to figure out what the hell he was talking about.

In between his mutterings about "no fucking chemistry between them," I figured out that he'd been taping wannabee actors who'd answered his cattle call for "long-term couples willing to 'bare it all' living out their sexual fantasies for the camera." Apparently, the results had been less than stellar.

Now, Marco was out of time. In fact, he was desperate enough that he was offering my partner and me a percentage, on top of our usual rates, if—big emphasis on the "if"—we could do a scene together hot enough for him to ditch the other footage he'd already shot.

The whole deal sounded too good to be true, which made me suspicious. Not that I didn't trust Marco. But I'd worked with him enough to know he always had a hidden agenda. I rolled the empty can in my hands until he finally slowed down enough for me to get a word in. Then I said, "I don't get it."

He stopped pacing and quirked an eyebrow at me.

"There's no script. We just have sex the way we do at home. If we do the scene hot enough, you pay us a bundle. What's the catch?"

"No catch, pal!" Marco grinned as he walked up next to me and slapped me on the back. "I film you and Jeff getting it on—you know, real porn stars having real sex." He winked at me. "It's the ultimate voyeuristic fantasy! If you make the scenes really hot—bump up sales enough to justify the startup costs—I can use this as the pilot to open up a whole new line of candid videos. Your audience gets to jerk off watching, you get one helluva bonus, the studio gets rich. Everybody's happy."

Suddenly, Marco grabbed my shoulder and turned me around, narrowing his eyes as he looked at my butt. "What the fuck is this? Did that asshole give you a hickey just before a shoot? I'll kill him!"

"It's a bruise. The makeup must have worn off." I pulled away, batting my eyes innocently. "I got it when Jeff and I fell out of bed, fucking. Does that make you feel better?"

"Ouch. Kinky, though." He smirked, then his eyebrows narrowed. "You guys do that often?"

I could almost hear the wheels turning, and I did not want to go down that road. I tossed my empty can in the trash.

"Every day," I smiled. I didn't have the heart to tell Marco that after a long day of fucking for money, my boyfriend and I liked to relax at home. We read, worked out together, watched movies with plots—slept! Our private lives did not revolve around a social whirl of orgies and anonymous tricks in the bars of West Hollywood.

Not that Marco would have believed that. He snickered, turning away as he waved the gaffer over to him. "We'll talk more when we're done today." He paused. "But give me a teaser. What would John Doe on the street need to do to have a sex life as hot as yours?"

"Marry Jeff Evans," I grumbled. I grabbed my dick and started stroking, ignoring Marco's laughter as I walked out of the room to get ready for my next scene.

Jeff was due home from his latest European shoot in two weeks. I knew I'd be horny as hell for him by then. But I wasn't looking forward to Marco's little project. Even though I was half of an "internationally famous" porn-star couple, I relished my private time alone with my lover. To my way of thinking, we didn't get enough of it.

Other than the one-take "you-suck-me-I'll-suck-you" jail scene where we'd met, Jeff and I hadn't done any movies together. I worked mostly in the United States. Popularizing cocksucking with condoms was my claim to fame. Jeff worked more overseas. Having a thick, uncut, country cock—and being able to speak Czech as fluently as his never-adjusted-to-Omaha mother—gave him an instant in with American companies who were capitalizing on the burgeoning East European markets. Jeff looked Slavic. He could talk to his costars as well as to the director. And he had one fucking gorgeous body.

Okay, so I'm biased. After five years together, Jeff's smile can still make my dick drool. Anybody watching a video of his can see how much he's enjoying himself. This is no straight man pretending to be gay. Jeff loves fucking ass. His beautifully tapered nine inches are thick as a beer can, and he's always hard. So, he's always cast as a top—even though he's so big it's sometimes difficult to find bottoms for his fuck scenes.

We get asked, often, what keeps us together. "You're both tops. Isn't it, you know, kind of pointless?"

Jeff's stock answer is, "I married him for his mind." At which time he grabs my crotch and winks at our interrogators. His squeezing always has the expected result. It's a good thing I like being hard in public.

What he doesn't say is that when it's just the two of us, we bottom to each other. I'm as long as he is, though not as wide, and I'm cut. Directors love the way my wide-rimmed mushroom head looks popping in and out of lips and assholes. The definition stays clear even when I'm inside the rubber. The PR folks say that complements what they call my "chiseled Greek looks." I have to admit, my dick does look good—even more so on a wide-screen TV.

Jeff loves working that rim with his tongue. He gives a mean blow job. I shoot geysers when he's doing me. Okay, so I'm also in love with the guy. He's well read, intelligent, prone to pulling practical jokes, and I've gotten used to sleeping with his prong poking me in the kidney all night. Besides, I love playing with his dick. His cum tastes great and he's got enough foreskin for the both of us.

That's what was going to be hard to explain to Marco—the skin part. At work, everyone we suck or fuck is always sheathed in latex. Jeff and I have both eroticized condoms to the point that just hearing a wrapper being torn open makes us stiff. But at home, we're body-fluid monogamous. A couple of years ago, after another round of negative tests, we'd decided that as long as we used condoms with everyone else, every time—and as long as there were no accidents—we'd go skin to skin with each other.

I didn't know how that was going to fit into Marco's grand marketing plans. He was adamant that he wanted to film us on Jeff's first night back from Europe—before we'd had a chance to fuck. After several long and very expensive phone calls, Jeff and I decided ol' Marco was going to get exactly what he'd asked for. We'd burn that bed up with the hottest action our illustrious director had ever seen. And for our troubles, Jeff and I were going to walk away with the money we needed for the balloon payment on our condo.

On the day of the shoot, Marco was in his usual rush. "What kind of props do you need?"

Jeff snickered and rubbed his crotch, the sizeable erection tenting the front of his robe. Despite his jet lag, after three weeks apart, we'd have been happy humping on the carpet.

"A couple towels, three or four pillows, some coconut massage oil." I shrugged.

"I want a second sheet and a blanket at the bottom of the bed."

I raised my eyebrows at my hot and horny partner's requests, but Jeff just smiled and kept rubbing his crotch. I reached over to help him.

"You got it." The ever-efficient Marco snapped his fingers and somebody was on it. His crews are always good. "Condoms, lube, the standard kit will be on the nightstand."

Jeff and I sat on the edge of the bed, ignoring him and the flurry of activity around us as we turned our concentration to necking and stroking the erections poking out through each other's robes.

"Zak, Jeff...*now*, please!"

We came up for air, gasping as we made a pretense of composing ourselves. I kept my hand in Jeff's lap, though. I couldn't quite bring myself to let go of him. I'd missed him.

Marco grabbed a fresh cup of coffee from his latest twink assistant and kept right on talking, like he actually thought we were listening to him. "Do whatever you want—fuck, suck, jack off. Just make it hot. And stay on the bed so we don't have to screw around with the lights."

He looked away, wincing as he sipped the steaming liquid. "We'll do the voice-overs later, as well as specific questions about your relationship and so forth, based on the action. Don't worry about that now." He stopped and looked at us over the edge of his cup. "Unless you have questions, we'll start in fifteen minutes."

When Jeff and I both shook our heads, Marco turned his attention back to the crew, and Jeff and I went off to finish getting ready. Marco assigned us each a minder, though, to ensure we didn't sneak off for a quickie somewhere. He wasn't going to let anybody disrupt his grand plans.

"Leave them alone! I will personally shoot anyone who interferes with what I expect to be record cum shots!"

Jeff and I knelt on the bed, facing each other, and handed our robes to the disappointed fluffers.

"Places everyone. Make me proud." Marco launched into his standard routine, and we were rolling. Jeff winked at me, giving my thigh a quick prod with that monster cock of his. I wiggled my eyebrows back at him. Then we took each other's hands and I let the techies' discussions fade away into the background. Just knowing they were there was all the encouragement my exhibitionist streak needed.

I was almost too worked up, though. I backed off until just my fingertips were touching Jeff's. Getting used to him again. Letting down my defenses. Letting him in. We didn't talk. Marco could damn well dub in music later.

Eventually, Jeff pulled my hand to his lips and sucked on my index finger, running the edges of his teeth sharply over my skin. When I shivered, he bit.

I don't know which of us moved first. One minute his mouth was hot and wet on my finger, the next we were kissing. I fell or he pushed me back on the bed—probably a little of both. Then we were rolling around on the sheets, groping blindly for each other, our dicks pressed together between us. I opened my mouth to breathe and sucked in his tongue.

"Damn, but I missed you, Zak."

I shivered as he licked over my teeth.

"You are the hottest man on the face of this fucking earth!"

"Shut up and kiss me," I growled, shoving my tongue down his throat.

We were too turned on for refinements. When Jeff started licking my ear, I twisted around and latched on to a nipple. That had the expected result. My country boy threw me flat on my back and straddled me—his fat, juicy cock snuggling right up against my lips. He positioned himself over me, on his knees and elbows, his legs widespread so he could lower himself onto my face. Then Jeff pulled my legs up and back so he had access to everything he wanted. Marco always liked sixty-nining. He was damn well going to get it today.

About two seconds later, I decided Marco was an idiot for not letting us come at least once before the cameras started rolling. My skin felt like it was reaching toward Jeff everywhere we touched. I fought not to shoot as he rubbed his face against my crotch. I gasped, wiggling as Jeff kissed the head of my dick. It was almost more than I could stand.

I tugged on his balls, trying to distract myself by licking his scent from them. It didn't help. It only made me want him more. His velvety shaft brushed against my cheek, teasing me. I opened my mouth. Using just my lips, I tugged his foreskin down over the slippery head. A drop of tangy juice oozed onto my tongue.

"Mm. You taste good," I whispered, carefully licking the sticky precum into my waiting mouth.

As my tongue swiped over his piss slit, Jeff cried out, bucking and gasping against me. In his next breath, with no warning at all, he sucked me deep into his throat.

I didn't expect it. I jerked back as my whole body convulsed. "Stop!" I gasped. "*Now*! Fuck, man, I'm gonna shoot!"

"Camera three, you better be getting this!"

Jeff froze, and I panted—ignoring Marco's comment and his muttering that we definitely hadn't given him enough footage yet. I clenched the muscles in my arms, concentrating on the details of the condo mortgage, on how nice Marco's clipboard would look shoved up his ass, trying to will myself back under control.

"Give me a second," I whispered.

"Whatever you say, lover." Jeff had taken his mouth off my dick, but he couldn't seem to quit touching me. Pretty soon, his hand moved to my perineum. He started stroking, gently at first, then more firmly, gradually moving down, touching, rubbing. He drooled spit onto me—lubing the way for his fingers. By the time I finally got my breathing halfway under control, Jeff was playing with my asshole. He kept my legs spread wide, so the cameras could catch the way he was stroking me—the slow, lazy, slippery circles.

When he slipped the tip of his finger into me, I moaned and gave it up. I knew right then how the rest of the scene was going to go. Jeff's fingers were talking directly to my asshole. I opened my mouth and took the tip of his cock between my lips—kissing him, working the soft, warm hood over the glistening head, tugging gently on his smooth, heavy balls. We were too far gone to go slowly. If Marco wanted more cinematic buildup, he could damn well edit it in later.

Jeff lifted up, sliding his finger down my thigh. "Roll over, Zak."

I did. When I was on all fours over him, Jeff stuffed a pillow under his head. I spread my legs wide and dropped down until just the tip of my cock rested on his lips. I hoped the cameras were getting everything they needed, because I wasn't about to budge for anyone but Jeff. And he had me right where he wanted me. He put his hands on my hips and pulled me down toward him. Then his hands were on my asscheeks, massaging them, spreading them wider. My cock fell forward onto his neck as I felt the featherlight touch of his breath caressing my asshole.

"Mm. This pretty pink pucker looks good, Zak. Real good."

I groaned, jumping at the first touch of his tongue. It was hot, it always is. He licked the edge of my crack, wetting skin that usually doesn't see daylight, especially not in my movies.

I nuzzled my cheek against his cock, kissing him, inhaling his scent. I wanted to let him know how much I appreciated his touch. Then I rested my face on his thigh, facing camera two, and focused all my attention on my asshole, just the way I knew Jeff wanted me to.

I didn't try to control my reactions. I'm not dignified in bed. Not in real life. I moaned as Jeff rimmed me. He licked up and down my crack. I gasped the way I always did when the tip of his tongue flicked over my asshole. I knew what was coming. I wiggled my ass at him, asking for it—begging. Loud and slutty. I didn't care who saw me. I hoped the cameras were catching every whorish grind for posterity.

Jeff stuffed spit up my hole. His fingers held me wide open, stretching my sphincter. Each touch of his tongue let him slip that much farther in. My asslips fluttered, reaching back for him as he kissed and sucked. He licked farther into me, caressing the inner skin, way inside, where the smooth surface was usually puckered tightly closed. With each step, he stretched me wider.

"You ready, babe?"

"Uh-huh," I gasped. I didn't care who heard the great porn star's boyfriend calling him "babe." My ass was hungry.

"You know what I'm going to do." He sucked, hard, on the outside of my hole. "You ready?"

I shuddered, nodding against his cock, unable to speak.

"You taste so good, babe." He kissed my asshole. "Here it comes."

I yelled when his tongue sank into me. I mean, Jeff dug his hot, nasty tongue into my ass and he ate me. He tongue-fucked my hole until I was almost screaming. Harder, deeper, hotter, he spread my cheeks so far apart it felt like my skin was splitting. I pushed back against him, grunting, bearing down, opening my asshole to him as he slurped. I didn't care what I looked like. My asslips kissed his tongue like it was his cock.

I cried out as he pulled away. He pushed me over onto my back, still sixty-nining, pressing his cock against my lips. I sucked him greedily into my mouth, inhaling the slippery, salty tang where the precum leaked out of his bunched foreskin.

"That's it, lover," he growled, thrusting into my mouth. His cock got longer, growing against my tongue. "Get it hard and get it wet. You know where it's going."

He was already like a rock, but I sucked, opening my jaw

wider as his shaft thickened and stretched even farther. His bared head was completely out of the foreskin now, the sensitive crown pressing against my tonsils, his cock filling my mouth. I breathed in through my nose, and as my lungs filled, Jeff thrust, gently, against the back of my throat. I tipped my head and opened to him, gagging as he slipped in deep. It was like trying to swallow a baseball bat. He shook—I love feeling him quiver, even when I'm suffocating. Then he pulled up and settled against me, his breath ragged, his cock resting above my mouth where I could play with it at my leisure—where the camera could catch every wet lick of me working the folds of his skin, sticking my tongue in his piss slit, sucking his low-hanging smooth balls until they were pink and slippery.

In spite of his shivers, Jeff pulled my legs up and back. He braced his elbows on the bed, his biceps against the backs of my thighs. It was a perfect ass shot. I was spread wide and my hole was open. Virgin ground for Marco's cameras. I heard the click of the bottle cap, smelled the coconut. Then Jeff's oiled hands glided over my cheeks. He smoothed the side of his hand up and down my open crack, brushing over my hole, gradually concentrating on rubbing my hungry, grasping sphincter. His fingers started stretching me.

"I want you nice and loose," he purred. "Show me how your asshole opens for me."

"But Zak's a top!" someone protested loudly in the background.

"Not today," Jeff snickered as he put one hand on each cheek. His index and middle fingers pulled me open. With each stroke, his fingers reached in farther. He kept pulling, stretching me wider, until my whole world was my asshole. I groaned as he kissed the inside of my thigh, his finger once more sliding over my asslips.

"You like?" I could feel his smile as he breathed against my leg.

"Fuck, that feels good," I gasped, sucking hard on his monster dick, taking it as deep in my throat as I could.

He laughed, shivering as I swallowed against him. This time, when his finger went in, it dug deep. I groaned, long and loud, feeling the familiar jolt as he found what he was looking for.

"What have we here?" He rubbed again. I could hear the smirk in his voice. "Somebody wants his joyspot massaged?"

He pressed hard and I cried out, an ooze of precum moving up my cocktube.

"Fuck, yeah, Jeff. Fuck, that feels good." I tried to arch against him. "Do it again, please!"

This time, his laugh gave me goose bumps. "I will, lover." I groaned as he rubbed, harder. "But I'm going to massage it with something designed specifically to make your slutty ass purr."

He pulled his hand out. My nose twitched as the smell of coconut again filled the air. I jumped as I felt the nozzle against my asslips. His fingers pulled my asslips open, then the cool oil trickled into me, deep down into my hole, lubing it, getting it slippery wet.

"Jeez, man, that stuff is gonna wreck the rubber." The techie's voice sounded far away.

I was too far gone to even laugh. I sucked harder on Jeff's cock, getting it wetter, getting it stiffer for where it was going to go.

Jeff moved off me, his dick making a wet, plopping noise as it popped out of my mouth. He pressed the oil bottle into my hand. Then he was between my legs, lifting my thighs up and back, spreading them wide. I bent my knees and he pressed them back toward my shoulders, tipping my ass high in the air.

"You ready, babe?"

This time I did laugh. The head of Jeff's cock was pressed into my asscheek—hot, demanding. I squeezed a huge puddle of oil into my hand, slathered the slippery grease over his cock, stroking, getting him even harder. I dropped the bottle next to myself and positioned him against me, rubbing his dripping dickhead against my hungry, hungry hole.

"Jeez, man, what are they doing?"

"Somebody give them a condom!"

"Damn, Jeff's *huge*!"

Jeff grinned down at me. I smiled back. As we'd expected, our audience was shocked.

My asslips fluttered against him, kissing him. I stroked his shaft, slicking the oil over him one more time, looking right into his hot, velvety eyes—velvety as his dick skin.

"Fuck me," I growled.

"Jesus, he's going in bareback!"

I don't know who said it. I didn't care. I cried out as Jeff's monster cock started crawling up my hole. They'd said to do it for real, and that's the way Jeff and I fucked each other—only each other. Bareback.

"Marco, do you see what they're doing? Fer chrissakes, stop them!"

I gasped as Jeff pressed into me. It burned; oh, god, it burned. It always did. Jeff's dick was so big and so thick and so fucking, fucking hard. I panted, keeping my mouth open, bearing down, willing myself to relax as my asslips stretched. I felt like I was being split in two. It hurt and it burned and, fuck, I wanted it.

"Damn, that's hot." Whoever said it was completely out of breath.

I knew we looked good. I lifted my head, watching Jeff impale me.

"I love watching my cock fill your hole." Jeff's words came

out through gritted teeth. He was making himself go slowly, trying not to hurt me—trying not to come.

I gasped as he slid in another inch. My asslips stretched—thinner, tighter.

"That's it, lover. Loosen up and take it all." He gasped, shuddering, as the sound of his voice seemed to open my hole. "God, you feel good! Unh!"

My sphincter relaxed in a rush, and Jeff slid in to the hilt. I lay back down, taking deep breaths, willing my body not to shake, not to panic at the sheer size of the cock buried deep in my rectum.

"Easy lover." Jeff's thumbs stroked the backs of my thighs. He was breathing hard, holding himself still over me. "It'll be okay in a minute. I'm gonna make you feel so good."

The pain passed, slowly, the way I knew it would. Gradually I became aware of another pressure, of the hard cock nuzzling against my joyspot. Pressing precum out of me. I looked up at Jeff. His face was flushed, his shoulders and arms and chest glistening with sweat. My cock twitched at the sight of him. I felt the jolt all the way around my asshole.

"Do it, you prick." I clenched my rectal muscles around him. "Fuck my horny ass until I come."

Jeff grinned. He leaned over and kissed me, shoving his tongue deep in my mouth. I sucked, hard. My asslips kissed his cock, matching the rhythm of my mouth.

He closed his eyes and pulled back. His smile turned to a gasp, then to a grimace. "Damn, but you're tight."

The friction still burned, but at the same time it felt so good. So damn good. Then he was in again. And out. And in.

"You ready?" Jeff pressed hard, grinding his pelvis against me, his balls heavy against my asscheeks as he once more looked down into my eyes.

I grappled on the bed for the bottle, slathered oil on my hand. Then I grabbed ahold of my long, hard porn-star cock and growled up at my panting lover. "Show me what you've got, fucker."

"Asshole," he snapped.

I yelled as Jeff shoved into me. Then he started fucking me, wild and fierce, his balls slapping against me. I cried out each time he punched my joyspot. I could tell I wasn't going to last long. Each time he hit my prostate, I surged closer, my juices boiling, ready to erupt. Ready to explode. I jacked myself faster, trying to match Jeff's rhythm. With each stroke I pulled waves of pleasure through my ever-expanding dick.

"Gonna come," I gasped. I shuddered as my hand stroked up. "Fuck me. Harder." My balls pulled up, tight. "Fuck me—dammit, *hard!*"

Jeff slammed his hips into me, punching into my joyspot—just the way I'd begged him to, just the way he knew I loved it. My hole clenched, hard and greedy. Then I howled as the orgasm washed over me. My dick and my prostate and my asshole became one continuous scream of pleasure. My cum spurted out and I yelled until my throat hurt.

It was a helluva money shot. The wet splats landed on my chin and my neck and my tits. The last couple on my belly. Jeff ground his hips into me, twitching his dick inside me until I swear every drop of sperm in my balls shot out my cocktube. I shook like my bones were breaking.

I was totally wiped out. As my hand stilled, I looked up. Jeff was balanced over me, his arms shaking, his breath erratic, sweat dripping down onto me. His face was a mask of concentration as he arched his cock into me, prolonging my pleasure.

My arms trembled as I reached up and grabbed his tits. "I love you," I panted. I pinched, lightly. "You are one hot fuck."

Jeff gasped, his eyes glazing. We were the only ones in the world. My hole was raw and sore and stretched so loose it felt like it would never be tight again. I didn't care.

I smiled up at him, twisting the hard little nipples between my fingers. "Fuck me, lover."

Jeff's cry was incoherent as he started thrusting into me again, pounding toward his climax. His dick slurped in and out of me, wet and sloppy. I tried to tighten for him. I managed a light twitch before my muscles gave out. He felt it—he shivered.

His cock ravaged my asshole with fast, deep, full strokes. I tugged hard, rhythmically, on his tits. His breathing was so fast, I knew he was right on the edge. I lifted my hips, taking him as deep as I could, rocking back as he bottomed out, as his body stiffened.

"You fucker," I gasped, an evil laugh deep in my throat. He'd destroyed my hole. I was sore as hell and, damn, it felt good. I jerked hard on his nipples. "Do it!"

"Aargghh!" Jeff's roar almost deafened me. He buried himself balls deep, his whole body shuddering; his thick, hard cock pulsing, stretching, throbbing against my poor battered asslips.

"Get ready, this is gonna be one helluva shot..." This time I distinctly heard Marco's voice in the background mix. "When Jeff pulls out..."

"Um, it's too late, Marco."

"What?"

"Jeff just came up Zak's ass."

"What? Nobody does that! Jesus H. Christ!"

"I'm not shittin' ya man, look! Jeff's whole ass is twitching."

"Jeff? Zak? Where's the cum shot?"

"Man, I just came in my pants—and I'm straight!"

"Dammit! Where's my money shot? Zak? Jeff? Where's my fucking money shot?"

Marco's curses degenerated into Italian. I tuned him out as Jeff collapsed on me. Jeff's breathing was ragged. He kissed me, clumsily missing my lips, then connecting. I lowered my legs and wrapped them around his waist, holding him to me in a ferocious bear hug.

Jeff pressed against me for a long time, his breathing slowly returning to normal. Finally he started to wiggle against me, his shoulders moving as he laughed into my neck.

"You liked?" He kept his voice low, just barely loud enough for me to hear.

I whispered back. "I'm gonna need diapers, you asshole. Damn, you're good."

He sucked on my neck. I could tell he was giving me a hickey.

"We gave them one helluva show."

When he could finally stop laughing, Jeff rolled off me, his dick pulling free with a loud plop. I reached down between my legs and felt my hole. It was puffy and sticky and about as well-used as a bottom boy's hole can be. I knew it would be back to normal by morning—it always was. But for now, my butt positively purred.

Jeff grabbed the extra sheet and the blanket from the bottom of the bed and pulled them over us. Then he spooned himself up against my back and wrapped his arms around me. I clenched my butt muscles, enjoying the stretched feeling and the sticky, tacky pull of his drying cum on my skin. The movement caused another trickle to leak out of my asshole and run down my leg. I shivered and pressed back against my lover, against his—for once—softly heavy cock.

"What are you two doing now?" Marco was beyond exasperation. He sounded genuinely perplexed. "What the fuck do you do for an encore?"

"We're rolling over and going to sleep," Jeff growled. "Just like in real life. Now shut up."

"Oh, fer chrissakes!"

Something heavy hit the floor. It sounded like Marco's clipboard. Then somebody started laughing—a lot of somebodies.

I closed my eyes and smiled as Jeff's breathing deepened. I knew we'd be getting our percentage. Marco was too greedy not to use a scene like we'd just given him. Jeff started to purr. I drifted right behind him. Marco's video was going to be great. And Jeff and I were even getting paid to sleep.

THE LOCKER-ROOM SCENE

Shaun Levin

I see the two Spanish guys first, but with him I take my time. No need to hurry. Not exactly a Nubian prince, him being a man in his midfifties, here in the changing rooms of the public swimming baths at the sports center at the top of Holloway Road. I've just walked in from the gym and there they are, all three of them naked. The two Spanish guys—beautiful in their own right—talking softly between them, but their gaze is on him, their bodies lean and tall, dark sprinklings of hair on their chests. One of them is using the locker next to mine and he stands so near I can see the soft hairs on his arse cheeks, the way they grow thicker toward the crack. His back is slim, streamlined. They head for the showers. But the black guy takes his time. He has, not long ago, emerged from the pool, then showered; now he towels himself near his locker, one leg up on the bench so that his thick circumcised cock pendulums between his legs, parallel to the leg he's balancing on as he rubs the light-blue towel between his thigh and scrotum. Soft cotton against smooth skin. As if there is no more than this audience of three. Vultures, hyenas, any animal, any beast hungry or in heat, nostrils flared for food and fucking. I am obliged to take note. To look. Because every now and then I am rendered breathless by a substantial cock glimpsed in a public place. Like him, I take my time: my shorts come off to expose the tattoo on the side of my thigh, a large bird in flight, then my T-shirt to show him, and them, too, my stomach, flat, yes, flat (I will shower at home). They move slowly, all of them. The light-brown men—to be called white, although at moments like this their identity is nothing, they know nothing of themselves, see nothing of their reflections, the only thought is their desire (our face is a hole, invisible to us, but public, scrutinized), a blinding truth, an engulfing need. Now, one of the light-brown men walks slowly toward his towel, his own towel that hangs on a hook attached to the other row of benches, opposite the bench where the man who is toweling himself, the dark-brown man who has not one drop of water left on his skin, continues to towel himself. And my tracksuit bottoms go on, my chest bare for them to look, the result of genetics and ritual, then a dry T-shirt. I'm covered. The Spaniards could be twins, light-brown men watching the dark-brown man. The other twin is still in the shower, his hand, his fist, his fingers stroking his thick light-brown cock. A shower scene on a loop: over and over washing his cock, rinsing it, soaping it, rinsing it. To the onlooker (me, but also not me, not me as I am now, my face a hole) these are two white guys and a black guy. One of them in the shower soaping his tubular uncut cock that hangs from a sparse bush of lathered, frothy pubic hair, a pipe, not hard, but definitely not soft. This is not the first time. I am twelve. I am ten. I am sixteen, closer to twenty, witnessing what should not be witnessed in public, should not be seen if we are to avoid becoming the animals we are bent on becoming.

The other one walks slowly, no thought of his own body, driven by a craving, bare feet on a wet floor, terra-cotta, ridged to avoid slippage. His everything is fixed on the black guy, who still towels himself. The roundness of his belly, the softness of his breasts—not soft…full, fleshy, not fat, he is *not* fat—but the two (all *three* of us!) care only about his cock. No, it is more than that (be precise): we follow the movements of his towel, the towel that moves, but does not leave his thighs, and always the cock is exposed. Everyone's is growing fatter. "They" being him and him, but they could be one, both of them with light-brown tubular uncircumcised penises, foreskins intact, weighed down by them, elongated.

I keep to myself, put my running shoes back on, feel sweat build up on my skin, sweating, but weak, weak from a cardio workout—I am not the audience. I came in after the scene had kicked off. I am not late, but I am too late to be part of it. I am neither the show nor the audience (which are one). The other two are audience; I am the audience beyond that. The one who is toweling himself is definitely not audience. In a room of three, the audience is in constant flux. But for now, the white guys are the audience. The one who performs, who stands, *still* with his leg on the bench, *still* with his small pale-blue towel between his legs—doing what he does for his audience of two (three), one *still* in the shower and one *still* walking slowly toward his towel (lime green).

A cat approaches a bird on the grass.

As if to say: I am performing a cannibal's dance, a hunter's dance, a predator's dance, a dance of prey—watch me! The man with the towel and his leg on the bench moves at the same pace, a dance slowed down, like in a Bill Viola video, like a dance of temptation, Bathsheba in the privacy of her roof garden, King David peering over the wall. To move any faster would break the spell, scare away the audience or invite attack. Pounce! It's all so fragile, it's hard to tell what will happen next.

He is in no rush to put on his underwear, but when he does they are clean and white, and they support everything he has. What is it about a substantial cock? I know men who like to look at big cocks in porn (pictures or movies); I very rarely watch porn, maybe now and again I'll go to the videos on XTube, but that's about it. Is it something to do with being blessed? Something men with big cocks have that the rest of us don't. Something hidden that only a select few get to see. Big cocks should not be on show. Seeing his thick cock between his legs in the locker room is breathtaking. I want to stare at a man who has been given something beautiful. By whom? God? Being close to a substantial cock can make one believe in God. Or luck. I had a lover who used to say my cock had magical qualities; he liked to suck it when he was on his knees looking up at me. His cock was bigger than mine, a cock that was perfect in every way. Very rarely do I feel inspired to go down on my knees. Now is one of those times.

Is it to do with entitlement? Are the feelings a substantial and unavailable cock invokes primal? Has it got something to do with impregnating women, how far one's penis can go into a vagina, farther than any other's, so that your semen will be the semen that gets to where it needs to get to first? The weight of his penis anchors him to the ground, gives him a stronger sense of here-ness in the world as he pulls up his jeans and buttons up his shirt and sits on the bench to tie his laces. And that's all I have to say for the moment about him. I will leave them there—a call from outside the changing rooms, for me, a young boy of ten, a man of forty, to come out already, to get the show on the road, because we're going home for dinner, and we don't want to be late. Again.

MY BEST FRIEND'S DAD

J. M. Snyder

The first man I ever fell in love with was my best friend's dad. Mikey didn't know about it, of course, and neither did Mr. Pierce.

The dad was nothing like the son. I'd known Mikey since kindergarten, when he pushed me off the swing set on the school playground and had to sit in time-out for the rest of recess. His dad had a hard voice: rough, burned out from too many late evenings with his friends huddled around the dining room table, cigarette smoke stinging their throats and watering their eyes as they played hand after hand of poker. Whenever I stayed over on one of those nights, Mikey and I were confined to his room upstairs, out of the way, though not out of earshot. The men's raucous laughter and coarse language made us envious. How I longed to have Mr. Pierce call me a dirty bastard one second, then clap me on the back and roar with approval at something I'd said the next.

Though most boys outgrew sleepovers once they reached

high school, I still stayed at Mikey's house a few nights every month. It got me out of my own home, and it gave me a chance to be close to Mr. Pierce, who probably never said two words to us on the nights I was there, but any small glimpse, any gesture, fueled my teenage crush. I wasn't too worried about the kids at school finding out I slept over at Mikey's, because we'd been friends for so long most people assumed we were a set. Wherever Mikey went, I wasn't far behind.

The last time I spent the night was the Saturday before I left for college. My mother had begun to get weepy whenever she saw me, sniffling into a tissue and babbling about losing her "baby boy." Please, I was eighteen, and the college I'd be attending was only a two-hour drive away, but to hear her tell it, I was practically taking classes on the moon. When Mikey called to see if I wanted to come on over, just for pizza and a movie, I couldn't pack an overnight bag fast enough.

Sleeping over at Mikey's meant an evening leafing through pornos, playing video games and watching horror movies on DVD. Mr. Pierce's poker buddies started showing up around six. While Mikey and I duked it out on one of his wrestling games for the Playstation and kicked the shit out of each other, I could hear the men downstairs laughing and cussing. As much as I liked Mikey's company, I wished I could join them.

We lost track of time. Finally Mikey tossed the controller aside and gave me a wicked grin. "How about you sneak downstairs and grab some beers out of the fridge?"

I gave him an incredulous look. "What? Hell, no. What if someone sees me?"

Mikey stood, stretched, and flopped sideways onto his bed, the springs creaking beneath his weight. Flicking up the bottom of his curtain, he craned his neck to look out at the street below. "Two of the cars are gone," he said as he rolled onto his back.

"It's kind of late. I think the card game's over. No one will see you."

"Your dad," I argued. I hadn't heard Mr. Pierce's heavy footsteps on the stairs, which meant he hadn't gone to bed.

But Mikey shrugged that off, too. "Probably passed out on the couch in the den. You'll be fine. Just go down, grab two bottles, and run back up here. If he sees you, tell him you're getting something to drink. He doesn't have to know what."

I still didn't want to do it, but I couldn't see any flaws in Mikey's logic or any reason why I *couldn't* do it without looking bad.

"Come on," Mikey cajoled. "What's he going to say? You probably won't even see him."

Pushing myself up on my feet, I announced, "I have to take a leak." I'd worry about the beers when I came back from the bathroom.

The moment I stepped into the hall, Mikey's braying laugh erupted behind me as he shoved the bedroom door shut. I heard the insidious *click* as he locked me out. Angry, I stormed across the hall into the bathroom and kicked the door shut behind me. "Asshole."

Looked like I was going downstairs after all.

I considered hammering on Mikey's door until he had no other choice but to open up. Then I figured Mr. Pierce would hear the commotion and come upstairs to yell at us, so I settled for hitting Mikey's closed door with my fist, which set him snickering inside the bedroom—I know, I heard him when I pressed my ear to the wood. "You're dead," I growled, my mouth against the doorjamb. "See if I bring you any beer."

"You better!" Mikey hollered. The closeness of his voice startled me—he was right on the other side of the door. I wriggled the knob but it didn't turn, which meant he held it tight to keep it from rattling. "You ain't getting back in here without at least two beers. One for each of us."

I waited, silent, until I could hear him breathing; he must've pressed an ear to the door, listening to see if I'd left or not. So I hit the door again, harder this time, and heard a satisfying "Ow!"

Before he could open the door to retaliate, I hurried down-stairs.

The first few steps disappeared quickly beneath my feet, but halfway down I paused. The darkness wasn't as complete as I had first thought. The lights in the living room were out, and if I moved a little to the left, I saw the kitchen was dark as well. But another step brought me closer to the bottom of the stairs, where I saw a warm glow of light spread in a small circle from the doorway where the living room and dining room met. As I crept closer, one step at a time, I realized that the folding louvered doors separating one room from the next had been pulled shut.

That gave me pause. The glow I saw came from under the door, where the wood was warped just enough that it didn't sit flush against the floor.

Straining to hear anything, I held my breath and listened. Someone cleared his throat, a discreet sound that told me Mr. Pierce was still in the dining room. Cards purred as he shuffled them, and a few poker chips clattered to the table as if he'd been stacking them out of boredom and they'd finally fallen over. But there was no other sound—no one talking to him, no nervous scuffling, nothing to indicate he wasn't alone in there. If he caught me...

At the bottom of the stairs, I peeked around the wall to get a good look in the kitchen. To my surprise, those louvered doors were also shut, though they didn't close all the way and the gap they left between the wall and the door allowed a shaft of light to penetrate the darkened kitchen. It illuminated an empty beer bottle that had been left on the counter so it cast an amber glow over the sink's faucet. If I were quick, I could probably sneak in there, open the fridge really slowly so it wouldn't make any noise, grab two bottles of beer and dash back upstairs before Mr. Pierce even knew I was there.

My socked feet were silent as I inched across the carpet onto the tiled floor of the kitchen. My heart hammered in my chest, every nerve was on end, and my hair felt puffed in fear all along my arms and the back of my neck. If I were caught...

I wouldn't be caught. In my mind's eye I could see myself getting the beers. I crept closer, watched my hand reaching for the refrigerator door, felt cool metal as my fingers closed around the handle. I wouldn't get caught. I *wouldn't...*

From the dining room came that sound again, half cough, half clearing the throat. With a voice steeped in gravel, Mr. Pierce spoke. "So you owe me what, three hundred?"

My hand froze on the handle. *Oh, fuck.* He wasn't alone.

I heard another sound, something sexy, a mingled laugh and moan. "Three-fifty. Don't round it down just because you're hard for me."

The words drew me closer. Without conscious thought, I relaxed my grip on the handle of the fridge and turned toward the partially shut louvered door. "*Hard* for me?" Was that what he had said?

Oh, Jesus.

I expected an angry shout, a denial, something fast and quick that sent this fellow packing. Instead, I was surprised to hear the hint of a smile in Mr. Pierce's voice when he answered, "I was cutting you some slack. I know you ain't got the cash."

With a throaty chuckle, his friend replied, "I know it's not cash you want from me."

I couldn't help it—my feet moved forward, heading for the louvered door. I stopped at the counter and tried to peer around the gap where the door and jamb didn't quite meet, but all I saw was blank wall. Were they talking about what I *thought* they were talking about? What I *hoped* they were talking about?

Then I heard muffled moans, a slight gasp, indistinct words. I inched closer and prized the louvers up slowly, careful not to let them squeak. Through the wooden slats I saw Mr. Pierce sitting at the head of the dining room table. He was turned toward me, facing a friend of his I recognized as RC, who sat on the bench closest to the kitchen, the same seat Mikey always preferred to use. Only RC wasn't exactly sitting any longer. Both hands leaned heavily on Mr. Pierce's thighs, rumpling the work pants he wore as RC fisted the dark blue material. RC stretched above Mr. Pierce, face buried in his neck, and as I watched, Mr. Pierce's thick lips parted in a low, guttural moan. One hand rubbed over RC's strong arm, kneading through his shirt. The other trailed down RC's chest to tug at the waistband of RC's jeans.

Suddenly my own jeans felt two sizes too small. Without thinking about it, I thumbed open the fly and felt the zipper part beneath the erection straining at my crotch. My whole body flushed at the sensation of my hard dick released from confinement and I pressed my palm against it before my fingers encircled my shaft through the cotton of my briefs.

When RC's mouth covered Mr. Pierce's, I bit my lower lip to keep from whimpering. *Yes,* I prayed. *Thank you, God, for letting me see this.*

Apparently Mr. Pierce didn't share my appreciation. With his hand flat against RC's chest, he held the younger man at bay. "Sweet as they are," he purred, "your kisses aren't enough to pay your debt."

"You're the one who knocked off fifty bucks." The coy smile

I heard in RC's voice excited me and I rubbed the front of my briefs, which had grown damp beneath my growing erection.

Mr. Pierce's laugh was like a warm hand that wrapped around my balls and squeezed gently. I almost moaned at the sound, but bit down harder on my lip to keep quiet. "I can get these for free whenever I want," he murmured.

The thought of these two men doing this—*this!*—after every card party with Mikey and me upstairs, ignorant, made me want to weep. I had never loved anyone as much as I did the both of them, right at that instant. Though I knew I should just tiptoe back up to Mikey's room without a word, before they knew I was there, nothing could force me to move. I wanted to see this, I *had* to see it.

My hand slipped into the waistband of my briefs. My fingers smoothed down the kinked curls at my crotch, then strummed along the stiffening length jutting from my unzipped fly. When my thumb rubbed over the tip of my cock, I whimpered a little with desire. Oh, hell yes. I needed this.

In the dining room, RC had folded one leg beneath him and now sat perched on the bench before Mr. Pierce, whose spread legs and slouched posture looked like an invitation I knew I would have never been able to resist. With sure hands RC explored the wide expanse of Mr. Pierce's chest, flattening his undershirt flush against his flesh. At the waistband of his pants, RC untucked the shirt, plucking it free from the belt buckle, and flicked it up to expose a pale swath of stomach. My fist tightened around my cock at seeing the hair swirled around his navel, black and gray as if seasoned just right; the slight paunch from the way he sat, the hint of belly fat that pooched over the top of his belt, the way the skin seemed to quiver when RC's fingers tickled over it. Leaning down, RC pressed his face to Mr. Pierce's stomach and rested his cheek in the tufts of hair as he snuggled close.

Jealousy flooded me. *I* wanted to be there, held in the safety of Mr. Pierce's embrace, clutched tight to the man I had loved all these years. My cock ached at the thought of doing that, *just* that, and nothing else. I stroked myself as I watched RC's lips pucker and kiss Mr. Pierce wherever he could reach without moving—belly, navel, the underside of one pectoral muscle that peeked out from beneath the shirt.

Pressing his mouth against Mr. Pierce's skin, RC suddenly blew a wet raspberry, the sound loud and startling in the silence.

Mr. Pierce growled as he shoved RC back and wiped at the slobber on his stomach. "Come on," he muttered, sounding exactly like Mikey when my friend wanted me to do something and I was too busy being silly to comply. "Are we going to do this, or what? Because you can leave."

RC's hands found Mr. Pierce's belt buckle. The teasing grin on his face made my whole body flush. "You don't want me to go."

Mr. Pierce grunted in reply, but stayed silent. With expert ease RC unbuckled the belt and let it fall open, then unzipped the front of Mr. Pierce's work pants. I leaned forward, squinting through the louvers, holding my breath as one word tripped like a litany through my mind. *Please, please, pleasepleaseplease.*

He tugged open Mr. Pierce's fly, pushing the material down out of the way as he parted it. Dingy white briefs appeared in the gap, rising like dough over Mr. Pierce's erection. I had to grip the counter with my free hand as I fondled my dick, my underwear chafing now, my body trilling with desire. Gently RC rolled down the top of Mr. Pierce's briefs, and the large cock that swung into view was ruddy and veined and so goddamn *huge* that I squeezed my balls when I saw it. When RC leaned down to rub that thick length against his cheek, I wanted to rush in there, push him aside and take his place.

I wanted that to be *me.*

I watched, giddy and light-headed, as he wrapped his tongue around the base of Mr. Pierce's shaft. I wondered what such flesh tasted like—I pictured myself in that position, head in Mr. Pierce's lap, tongue buried in the graying hair of his crotch. It was *my* tongue I saw slide up the length of his cock, my tongue that swirled around the bulbous tip, my tongue that dipped down the dribbling slit before my mouth opened wide to take him in.

As RC went down on Mr. Pierce, I gasped. I pushed my underwear below my balls and squatted a bit, leaning back against the counter to get comfortable. My erect dick hardened in the cool air, my nuts hanging low between my legs, and I licked my palms, first one, then the other, before resuming massaging my own length. The spittle helped, easing the friction. My fingers flew over familiar territory as not five feet away, Mr. Pierce leaned back in his seat, a blissful smile on his face while RC sucked his cock. This was my daydream come true, my fantasies made real. It was me in there with him, my throat working his erection, my fist tight around the base of his shaft, my fingers rubbing under his scrotum to rim the hairy darkness at his core.

In all my eighteen years, I had never seen a man pleasured by another. Oh, I had seen pictures—those magazines under my bed had their fair share of cum-flecked and dog-eared pages, to be sure. But they were staged images, hard cocks that had been stroked and polished until they gleamed for the cameras. All the pinups were solo shots, not couples. I didn't Google gay porn online because the last way I wanted to come out to my family was by someone—my mother perhaps, or a teacher at school—discovering the websites I had visited recently. I knew gay porn existed; I just didn't have access to it. RC's kiss was the first time I ever saw two men show any affection toward each other that extended beyond a handshake or a clap on the back. So this, *this*—Mr. Pierce shoved deep into RC's willing mouth, one hand holding the back of RC's neck, the other cradling RC's unshaven cheek...this was my first glimpse of heaven.

After several long minutes, Mr. Pierce clenched his hand into a fist at RC's nape. The next time RC bobbed up, the hand on his face eased beneath his jaw, holding him back. The look Mr. Pierce gave RC smoldered—even across the distance that separated us, I felt that look deep in my groin and had to bite into the fleshy base of my thumb to keep from crying out with want. "Damn, you're good," Mr. Pierce said, his voice soft.

My cheeks blazed at the compliment as if it had been directed toward me.

A slow smile softened Mr. Pierce's stern features. "But you know what I want."

RC laughed and turned his face to press his mouth in Mr. Pierce's palm, planting a kiss there. "What you *always* want. A piece of my ass."

There was the slightest hint of a tease in Mr. Pierce's voice when he countered, "It's an oh-so-fuckable ass."

"You like it?" RC asked.

My mind whirled out in a blind rush. *Oh, god. Oh, my god. They aren't...they won't...please please please yes.*

In a seductive purr, Mr. Pierce admitted, "I love it."

My hand tightened around my aching dick. *Yes, yes, yes.*

In one fluid motion RC stood, hands opening his fly as he turned and shucked down his jeans. He bent over slightly, mooning Mr. Pierce and giving me a good look at those plump, dimpled cheeks. His ass was smooth and tanned, with a hint of dark hair curving beneath each buttock to trail into the crack between them. A mole sat like a beauty mark just below the tailbone on his right buttock, one single imperfection on an otherwise flawless canvas. "If you love it so much," RC joked, "why don't you kiss it?"

My whole body throbbed with need. *Yes.*

When Mr. Pierce leaned forward, his stiff cock poked his belly, the damp tip smearing the trail of hair below his navel. His large hands caught RC's hips, pulling the younger man closer; his lips puckered, straining forward as he aimed for RC's ass. His mouth closed over that small mole with a loud *smack!* I could hear from where I sat. My fingers flew along my dick, jerking it sore, seeking release as I panted, watching, wanting more.

As if he heard my silent plea, Mr. Pierce obliged. Spreading RC's buttocks apart, he licked out to taste the dark skin hidden between them. In fascination I watched that tongue wet a path down, *down*—I could almost feel it on my own ass, which trembled for such a touch. It'd be warm, and softer than a man had a right to be, the saliva cooling along my flesh almost instantly. Mr. Pierce buried his nose between those ripe mounds, his jaw widening as his tongue angled down between them. I saw that tongue flick in and out beneath RC's left cheek and could only imagine just where it tickled when out of sight.

All coyness had left RC's face. He now leaned heavily against the dining room table, both palms flat on cards and poker chips alike. His head was thrown back, a look of sheer ecstasy written on his features. "Yes," he panted, arching his butt into Mr. Pierce's face. His feet slid apart as he tried to spread his legs wider. "God, yes. Right there, Hank. That's it. That's the spot. *Jesus*. Right *there*!"

He leaned forward, forearms on the table now, standing on tiptoes as he presented himself to Mr. Pierce. With expert deftness, Mr. Pierce lifted RC's buttocks and separated them, allowing me a glimpse of the puckered hole like a delicious treat at his center. I could see the muscles flex, could feel the tongue rimming the tight bud as if it were *my* ass upon which Mr. Pierce gorged. Softly I mimicked RC's desire-filled cries as I pulled my cock toward release. "Yes, *yes*." When the tip of his tongue disappeared into RC's hole, I whispered Mr. Pierce's real name, "Hank."

A thrill went through me. It felt so wicked, and as a result the first dribble of precum slicked my hand.

From my angle, I couldn't see RC's cock. As Mr. Pierce explored his anus with lips and tongue, RC raised one leg and set his foot on the bench where he had sat earlier. His jeans, bunched at his knees, were now pulled taut between his legs. He pushed them down, out of the way, his boxers following suit, and I finally saw the long, hard dick standing up from the dusky patch of hair at his crotch. An easy ten inches, thin, it curved to the right and made me feel impossibly inadequate. With one hand, he reached down and tugged it toward the center of his frame as if trying to corral it into place, but it had a mind of its own and continued to pull to one side. I wondered what that felt like during sex—if he fucked me, would I feel it angling one way or the other inside my ass, or would my own body be enough to tame it straight? God, I wanted to know. I wanted to crawl into the dining room, hide beneath the table, and let RC shove that thick length into my tender hole as far as it would go while Mr. Pierce took RC from behind.

I would have given anything to be brave enough to join in.

Instead I continued to watch, biting the inside of my cheek as I pleasured myself. "Hank," RC sighed, over and over again. "God," and "yes," and "Hank, *Jesus*," as if this were a religious experience for him. I knew I was close to coming, and I wasn't the one on the receiving end of Mr. Pierce's relentless ministrations. How RC didn't shoot a load, how he even managed to *stand* when my own knees wanted to buckle, was beyond me.

Finally, RC gasped, "Hank!" Louder this time, almost a command, his voice breathless. "Enough already. Just fuck me, will you?"

With a last kiss on the mole that started it all, Mr. Pierce joked, "Oh, so *now* you're ready to pay the piper."

"I want your cock," RC said, his vulgar words enflaming my blood, "in my ass, in *two* seconds, or I'm going to spaz all over the table here and you can explain to the guys next time they're over why your cards are covered in my cum."

That earned him a smack across the ass, a sound that reverberated through me and left a red mark in the shape of Mr. Pierce's hand on one round cheek. "They won't know it's yours," he muttered. He stood, unzipping his pants farther and hitching them low on his hips. His dick was still ramrod hard, but he stroked it lazily as he rubbed the fat tip up and down the cleft between RC's buttocks. "Did you bring a rubber, or do you want to ride bareback this time?"

RC straightened as he reached into the front pocket of his jeans. "What happened to your supply?"

Mr. Pierce shrugged. "I don't know. Maybe the kid got into them, who knows? Maybe we used them all up last time."

"Maybe you used them on someone else," RC teased. Extracting his hand from his pocket, he tossed a couple of coin-shaped condom packets onto the table.

Mr. Pierce reached around RC, a hand sliding under RC's shirt to smooth across his belly. His cock pressed against RC's ass, pinned between them, as Mr. Pierce leaned over the younger man. With his mouth on RC's neck, he murmured something I strained to hear. "There's no one else but you."

God. Oh, god. That phrase alone would fuel many fantasies in the days to come.

I leaned forward, my face against the louvers now, my breath hot and damp where it blew back in my face. I wanted to see everything in excruciating detail but Mr. Pierce was quick—in seconds he had the condom open and rolled onto his dick. Frustration welled in me; I wanted to replay the scene, watch it again in slow motion, see play-by-play how the lubricated condom encased his sausage-like dick. I wanted to savor the foreplay—the ease of that thick shaft between RC's tight buttocks, the filling press of cockhead to anus, the sweet pain as RC took Mr. Pierce in inch by glorious inch.

But I blinked and missed it. I saw discomfort flit over RC's features, but by the time my gaze traveled down to where their bodies melded, Mr. Pierce was already inside, his hips thrust forward, his balls hanging over the waistband of his briefs. RC's ass dimpled as he flexed, guiding Mr. Pierce deeper. Then he leaned the top half of his body down on the table, ass in the air, as Mr. Pierce found a slow, steady rhythm between them.

I renewed masturbating, timing my strokes with Mr. Pierce's. I tried to get a better look—I wanted every single moment of this night etched in my memory. I needed it, needed this, and already treasured these few stolen minutes when I was witness to something transpiring between two men that was worlds more beautiful than I had ever dared hope. I scooted closer, wanting more.

The edge of my foot struck the louvered door.

For one heart-stopping moment, Mr. Pierce seemed to freeze. RC's head was on the table now, his cheek pressed to the poker cards still lying there, and I saw his eyes swivel toward my hiding place. Every ounce of my body screamed at me to run but I couldn't move, couldn't breathe, couldn't *think*. They knew. Oh, god, they knew.

Oh, shit.

But Mr. Pierce had transcended reality—all that existed for him was his lover, the muscle encircling his cock and whatever myriad of emotions had swept him away. His movements were steady, a constant rocking that drove him into RC's ass with a gentle pounding and a faint *uh uh uh* that escaped his parted lips. So that's why Mikey made that same funny little sound when I'd heard him jerking off under the covers. Mr. Pierce leaned over RC, hands flat on the table on either side of RC's body, pushing his hips against RC's padded ass. His eyes were shut, his cheeks slack, and he was fucking not only with his dick but with every fiber of his being, giving himself wholly to the moment and the man beneath him.

After a breathless second when I was sure RC had seen me through the partially closed slats, he too gave in to their coupling. His eyes glazed over and rolled back as he moaned in pleasure. I picked up my own rhythm again, matching Mr. Pierce's, tugging myself to release not once, not twice, but three exhilarating times, each orgasm racking me silently. They felt like a strand of pearls, each one precious, pulled from me in rapid succession. My palm filled with jism; I smeared it along my length, coaxing a second ejaculation from me, and a third.

Suddenly the scene before me seemed private, too intimate, and I felt ashamed for watching. Mr. Pierce leaned over RC almost protectively, grinding his hips into his lover. RC fucked into his own hand, fondling his balls, reaching down farther to toy with Mr. Pierce's behind him as well. Together they moved toward ecstasy, each guiding the other to a climax I knew would be as mind-shattering as my own.

I leaned back against the counter to catch my breath, my sore dick now limp between my legs, my feet and legs numb from the position I'd been in for so long. Rolling my head to one side, I saw the edge of a dishtowel hanging over the counter above. I reached up, stretching, and snagged it down. The faint smell of Dawn soap wafted up from the still damp rag, which I used to gingerly clean myself off.

In the dining room, RC's breath grew ragged. "Yes, yes," he moaned. Then, raising his voice, he cried out, "Yes! God, Hank, harder, fuck me, *harder.*"

Between clenched teeth, Mr. Pierce warned, "Shh. My son's upstairs."

"Harder," RC whispered. He pushed back against Mr. Pierce, eager to get off. "Harder, *harder.* Yeah. Oh, yeah. Yes, yes, *yes.*"

I saw Mr. Pierce's buttocks tighten inside his briefs. He thrust forward one last time, up on tiptoe now, and held that position as he threw back his head, a guttural moan rising from the back of his throat when he finally came deep within RC's ass. Mr. Pierce's orgasm triggered RC's own, and I saw a few white drops trickle down RC's wrist as he closed his hand into a fist to keep from dripping onto the floor. "God!"

Then Mr. Pierce collapsed onto RC's back. "God," he said again, his voice scratchy and hoarse with exhaustion. "You're something else, you know that? You're damn good."

RC turned his head slightly, lips pursed. "You ain't bad yourself, old man. Kiss me."

Without comment, Mr. Pierce did just that.

I blinked slowly, as if waking from a dream. A satisfying wet dream that had left me spent. I felt warm and relaxed, and if I had access to one of those packs of cigarettes left discarded on the dining room table, I would've lit up even though I'd never smoked a cigarette in my live. But I wanted to breathe in deep, hold in the moment; let it percolate within me, sear my lungs; then exhale slowly, sated. I felt as though *I* had just been the one in there, fucking, fucked. I had never found such release in masturbation before and knew, sadly, I probably never would again.

But now I knew how it could be between men, how wonderful and amazing it could be, and I looked forward to college more than ever. I wanted what I'd seen tonight, a man of my own, those kisses and that hard dick in my ass, that tight muscle encircling my cock. And I'd have it. The rest of my life spread out before me like a promise I planned to keep to myself.

All that and more.

Dazed, I pushed myself up off the floor and deposited the soiled dishcloth on the counter. With gentle fingers I tucked my now wilted member into the confines of my briefs, clammy from my own juices. I zipped up my jeans, careful to be quiet.

Hurrying to the fridge, I grabbed two bottles by their necks, then shut the door and hurried around the corner. I took the steps two at a time back to Mikey's room.

Outside Mikey's door I shifted the beers into both hands again and tapped the bottom of one bottle gently against the door. Pressing my face to the jamb, I whispered, "Mikey, it's me. I got the booze. Open up."

ABOUT THE AUTHORS

SHANE ALLISON's writings have graced the pages of dozens of journals and saucy anthologies; a poetry collection, *Slut Machine;* and a book-length poem/memoir, *I Remember.* He has edited more than a dozen gay erotica anthologies. He resides in Florida, where he is hard at work on his first novel.

MICHAEL BRACKEN's short fiction has been published in *Best Gay Romance 2010, Beautiful Boys, Black Fire, Boy Fun, Boys Getting Ahead, Country Boys, Freshmen, The Handsome Prince, Homo Thugs, Hot Blood, The Mammoth Book of Best New Erotica 4, Muscle Men, Teammates* and many other anthologies and periodicals.

DALE CHASE (dalechasestrokes.com) has been writing male erotica for more than a decade with numerous stories in magazines and anthologies. She has two story collections in print: *If The Spirit Moves You: Ghostly Gay Erotica*, and *The Company He Keeps: Victorian Gentlemen's Erotica.*

JAMIE FREEMAN (jamiefreeman.net) lives in the historic center of a small Southern town. His work is featured in *Best Gay Erotica 2009, 2010* and *2012, Hot Daddies, Blood Fruit* and *Special Forces*. He's hard at work on more erotic stories, so stay tuned.

DOUG HARRISON's stories appear in twenty anthologies. His memoir, *In Pursuit of Ecstasy*, is online. He was active in San Francis's leather community, and appears in videos and photo shoots, including the Bare Chest Calendar. He has grandchildren, a hunky partner and two tomcats. He lives in Hawaii.

DAVID HOLLY (facebook.com/david.holly2) is fascinated by the human penchant for odd mythologies, bizarre rituals, diverse religions, forlorn hopes and broken dreams. He is fond of strong coffee, red wine, English bitters, nude beaches and hot-looking guys. He wears bright colors, tight slacks, exotic underwear and slinky swim briefs.

THOMAS KEARNES's fiction has appeared in Storyglossia, PANK, JMWW Journal, Word Riot, Night Train, The Pedestal, LITnIMAGE, Knee-Jerk, The Northville Review, Underground Voices and the gay venues Blithe House Quarterly, Velvet Mafia, *Educe Journal, Best Gay Romance 2009* and *OMGQueer*. He recently published an e-book of his short fiction, *Pretend I'm Not Here*.

SHAUN LEVIN is a South African writer based in London. He is author, most recently, of *Trees at a Sanatorium* and *Snapshots of The Boy* , and of *Seven Sweet Things* and *A Year of Two Summers*. He edits the queer literary/arts journal, *Chroma*.

JEFF MANN has published three poetry chapbooks, three books of poetry, two collections of personal essays, two novels, a collection of memoir and poetry and a volume of short fiction. He teaches creative writing at Virginia Tech in Blacksburg, Virginia.

TONY PIKE's erotic fiction has previously appeared in *Vulcan* and *Zipper* magazines in the United Kingdom, and in the anthologies, *Dorm Porn II*, *Boy Crazy* and *Best Gay Erotica 2011*.

RON RADLE writes gay love stories from the heart of the South Carolina Bible belt. His work has been published under a number of names in a number of places, both literary and nonliterary. He is finishing an erotic romance novel set during his college days in the mid-1980s.

ROB ROSEN (www.therobrosen.com), author of the novels *Sparkle: The Queerest Book You'll Ever Love*, *Divas Las Vegas* and *Hot Lava*, has contributed to more than 125 anthologies, most notably *Best Gay Romance 2007*, *2008*, *2009* and *2010*.

DOMINIC SANTI (dominicsanti@yahoo.com) is a former technical editor turned rogue whose stories have appeared in many dozens of publications, including *Hot Daddies*, *Country Boys*, *Uniforms Unzipped*, *Caught Looking*, *Kink* and several volumes of *Best Gay Erotica*. Future plans include more dirty short stories and an even dirtier historical novel.

J. M. SNYDER (jms-books.com) writes gay erotic/romantic fiction and has worked with many different publishers over the years. Snyder's short stories have appeared in anthologies by Alyson Books and Cleis Press. In 2010, Snyder founded JMS

Books LLC, a queer small press, which publishes GLBT fiction, nonfiction and poetry.

MARK WILDYR's (markwildyr.com) short stories and novellas, more than fifty and counting, have appeared in the magazines *Freshmen* and *Men* and in anthologies from assorted publishers, among them Alyson, Arsenal Pulp and Cleis, Companion, Green Candy, Haworth and STARbooks. *Cut Hand,* his full-length historical novel, was published in 2010.

ABOUT THE EDITOR

RICHARD LABONTÉ (tattyhill@gmail.com), when he's not skimming dozens of anthology submissions a month, or reviewing one hundred or so books a year for Q Syndicate, or turning turgid bureaucratic prose into comprehensible English for the Inter-American Development Bank or the Reeves of Renfrew County, Ontario, or coordinating the judging of the Lambda Literary Awards, or crafting the best croutons ever at his weekend work in a Bowen Island recovery center kitchen, likes to startle deer (while watching out for the alleged cougar and stepping gingerly over bear scat) as he walks terrier/schnauzer Zak, accompanied by his husband, Asa, through the island's temperate rain forest, where he has lived for several years, after managing gay bookstores in LA, SF, and NY from 1979 to 2000. In season, he fills pails with salmonberries, blackberries and huckleberries. Yum. Since 1997, he has edited almost forty erotic anthologies, though "pornographer" was not an original career goal.